American Diaries

AMELINA CARRETT
BAYOU GRAND COEUR, LOUISIANA, 1863

———∞∞∞———

by Kathleen Duey

———∞∞∞———

Aladdin Paperbacks

For Richard
For Ever

First Aladdin Paperbacks edition April 1999

Aladdin Paperbacks
An imprint of Simon & Schuster
Children's Publishing Division
1230 Avenue of the Americas
New York, NY 10020

The text for this book was set in Fairfield Medium
Printed and bound in the United States of America
10 9 8 7 6 5 4 3 2 1

ISBN 0-689-82402-5

October 14, 1863 My seventeenth day alone.

Nonc Alain will hold me to my promise, I know, so I will write in this silly book again this morning. The unfairness of it is clearer to me as time passes. He himself cannot read or write, but he insists that I learn from Father Le Blanc, and that I practice every single day. Nonc Alain says paper is rare now, with the war, that I am fortunate to receive this gift from Father Le Blanc. Ink, he says, is even more scarce since the Yankees have closed the port at New Orleans. He says I should be grateful. I see it just the other way. Better to give this paper to someone who wants to write. And the ink and the pen. I asked for none of it.

I have little to say this morning. Less than yesterday when I wrote about the *bal du maison* at Marie and Anne Legendre's place—and the gumbo Grandmère Magdelaine made for us all. She cannot read or write, either one, and she is happy in her life, as are her daughters and sons, many of them grown and married already—who also cannot read or write!

This pen hurts my hand and yet I have filled barely half a page. What else can I tell about?

Nothing!

I can say this much . . . Writing is a chore worse than cleaning the pig slops. This is nonsense, this aimless writing in a book about nothing much at all. I have been asking whether people can write lately. Margarite Bossiere does not read or write. Nor does Tante Rosemarie, and she is a traiteur who heals many people and is loved by everyone. Nor did my father or mother when they were alive. My mother taught me her English, so I can speak two languages—Nonc Alain's English is terrible, though he thinks it is good. Perrine cannot speak it at all. Most cannot. I am already different enough, am I not? No one on this bayou writes except old Simon Legendre—and Simon has told me he has almost forgotten how and does not miss it.

Still, Nonc Alain will not listen to me. He only says what Father Le Blanc says when we go to the masses he performs at Tante Leah's—write! write! write! I know why he insists. Father Le Blanc has convinced him I will make a life at Sacred Heart Convent—teach at the academy, become a sister. Nonc Alain likes the idea, I think, because then he would be free of his responsibility for me—and he would not have to admit to the rest of the family that he did not ever really want to take me in. He is wrong, though. I do not wish to live with twenty quiet old nuns—and teach writing and reading to all the noisy, spoiled daughters of every wealthy cane planter on Bayou Teche. Nor do I hear the call of God to become a nun—though I know that was my father's wish.

I am afraid to write what I really want . . .

I want to become a traiteur, like Tante Rosemarie—if she would ever think of passing her gift on to me. After all, she has grown daughters of her own—though none of them is left-handed. Most traiteurs are, as I am. And I do feel the strongest wish to help when I see someone hurt or sick. Tante Rosemarie does not speak to me of this. And I cannot raise the question, of course. I can just imagine Father Le Blanc's face if she does pass her gift to me. He does not approve of traiteurs, but he could not say much without making everyone here very angry with him.

I will see to the stock this morning, then gather moss again, with Perrine. There will be a boucherie this Sunday at Jean Hebert's maison. That means we will make boudin! I cannot wait. Not for the whole summer have I eaten sausage. Tante Honorine let me know about the party yesterday evening when I came past her place to tell Perrine we would be going this morning. She also said Nonc Jean told her the blue-coated soldiers are abroad again and coming up from the south. This could be worse than last spring when they came to take over the salt mine on Avery Island.

Tante Jasmine told me last Sunday that her husband has deserted from his officers once more. He says it is not our war and that this Confederate conscription is wrong. He calls the war la guerre des Confederes. I wonder if the Confederates think of this war as their own? Or the Yankees? Who would want a war to be their own?

And now, this makes the full page I pledged Nonc Alain. My promise is kept and done and I will go to do my work. I ought to hurry. Perrine said to come early.

CHAPTER ONE

Amelina lifted the pen, frowning. She thought for a moment about writing what was bothering her most—but she could not write it down, nor could she talk to Tante Rosemarie or Tante Honorine or anyone else about it. And of course she could say nothing to Nonc Alain. She had lived with him almost five years, since her eighth birthday, and in many ways she was grateful to him for taking care of her. But he made her angry at times, too, and lately he worried her. When he came back from his long journeys in his *bateau*, he brought odd things with him: a pure-blooded pig; a fancy clock; bolts of cloth for his sisters. These were things he had no money to buy. She could not imagine him stealing but—

Biting her lip, trying to put her mind on something else, Amelina tapped the steel pen nib against the paper. A fat drop of black ink gushed from the tip. Amelina stood up quickly, looking around the room for something to blot it with. If it had been up to her, she would have simply torn the page out, crumpled it, and thrown it away. But she had given her word to Nonc Alain about the writing and that was that. He would make her show him a page for each day, and she did not want to start over and write another. She shook her head stubbornly. No. The stain would stay if it must, but she would not write another page.

Amelina glared at the tiny ink puddle as it shrank, sinking into the paper. Impatiently, she stretched her fingers, releasing the pen cramps. Father Le Blanc had assured her every time he gave her a lesson that she did not have to grip the pen so tightly— but she could not make it do what she wanted it to do otherwise. The polished horn was slippery and always seemed to dance out of her control. Even holding it tightly, her letters had loops that were uneven—too wide, too narrow, slanting forward, then backward again.

Amelina frowned and pushed her hair away from her face. Her handwriting looked almost nothing like the priest's perfectly uniform penmanship. She could read it; she doubted if anyone else would ever be able to.

Amelina blew on the still shiny ink spot, then snapped the book closed, refusing to wait any longer. The ink would spread, staining one or even two adjacent pages before it had been absorbed completely. Nonc Alain would shake his head and shrug and explain that one did not have to be an educated man to know that blots were not acceptable. He had made the alligator skin cover for the book to protect the perfect cream white of the paper from the smears and grime of the household. He would not be pleased to see that stains and smudges could come from *within* the book itself.

"I promised I would write in this book," Amelina said to the smooth pine boards in the ceiling. "I did not say I would like doing it, or that I would improve at it."

She tossed the journal onto the foot of her bed. Then she patted at the homespun cottonade of her top mattress. It was time to air the lower mattress, she knew. It needed a good shaking so the corncobs would stay dry and not mold. But she would have to put it off for at least another few days. She had too many other chores to fit in.

Patting and fluffing the top mattress, pushing the lumps out of the thick layer of moss inside it, Amelina evened out the hollows and holes she had put in it over the course of the night. Then, she shook her pillow so the feathers wouldn't mat down.

Amelina straightened up, thinking about her cousin Perrine. She wouldn't awaken to silence and an empty house. Her brothers and sisters would be playing, their high-pitched voices coming from the yard outside her room.

Amelina sighed and blew out her little oil lamp. It was lonely without Nonc Alain. His constant whistling was as familiar to her as the sound of the birds in the oak trees. It bothered her that he was gone so much, but she knew better than to ask him about it. He would only shake his head and tug her hair and tell her to start the roux for supper. Then he would clean his gun while she browned the flour for the sauce and never say another word about what he was doing in Vermilionville or Grand Coteau or wherever it was that he had been going.

Amelina frowned. He often took muskrat and 'gator skins with him and returned with flour or sugar or coffee. But he was gone far too long for these trades to be the main reason for his journeys. And he had all but stopped farming over the past year . . .

Refusing to start another day by worrying herself, Amelina smoothed her bedcover, comforting herself with the touch of the soft cottonade her mother had woven. It calmed her the way paddling the bayou in her father's pirogue always did—making her feel like her parents were still close by. Then she opened the trunk that held the rest of her inheritance and allowed herself a moment of sadness as she looked at her father's clothes and her grandmother's Bible.

Closing the trunk firmly, Amelina faced the little statue of The Virgin that Nonc Alain had placed on a shelf above her bed to watch over her. Amelina lifted her hands and closed her eyes to pray for Nonc Alain's safety. He knew the bayous as well as any man, and his bateau was sound, thick cypress, made as tightly as any bucket. But still there were alligators and cottonmouths and soldiers and other dangers. Amelina added a short prayer that the war would soon end.

People were saying the Yankees had done more damage than a hurricane with all of their marching back and forth across the bayous and prairies, stealing hogs and yams and ruining farms.

"Bonjour! Fille? Bonjour!"

The voice startled Amelina. She didn't recognize it—and whoever it was spoke graceless, accented French. She ran out of her boudoir into the larger front room, then crossed it in six quick steps, her bare feet silent on the smooth plank floor, her soft cotton dress brushing her ankles. She pulled her bonnet from the pegged board above the pink settee and put it on as she went out, opening the front door wide. The homespun cotton touched her brow and covered the back of her neck.

Pausing on the *galerie* beside the steep stairs that led up to the loft, she looked out from beneath the wide roof. The sun was coming up and the line of cypress trees on the far side of the bayou sifted the sparkling light. No one was on the path.

Running lightly, her dress hitched up to her knees, Amelina raced toward the levee and topped it, looking down the gentle slope toward the bayou. There, on the dark, slow moving water close to the dock, was a man in a bateau, his hands loose on his oars as he glided to a halt on the almost still water. He had boxes piled up in the back of his boat.

"Come see," he called, raising one hand. The silvery notes of a *marchand*'s bell came across the yard. Amelina saw it twinkle in the sun. There was a rivulet of water coming from the raised oar. It caught the sunlight, too, and split it into a rainbow.

"Good morning, Ti' Amelina," the marchand called out, placing the words together like a child, slowly and deliberately. "Your Tante Rosemarie says you might be in need of some buttons." He gestured across the bayou to the north, at Tante Rosemarie's and Nonc Jean's house. Amelina followed his gesture and saw her aunt standing in her high garden, waving.

Amelina waved back, then looked downhill at the marchand again. She did not like strangers calling her by her nickname. It meant "little Amelina" and it was a leftover from the days when her mother was alive, coddling her as all mothers did. Even Nonc Alain didn't usually call her that. In this man's voice, the name sounded silly, unfamiliar.

"I have no money," Amelina called to him, frowning so he would know she was not a child to be won over with a peppermint stick or a wink. "Not Confederate scrip or Yankee," she added, to show him she understood something of the world. "No money at all."

"Do you have eggs?" He rowed one shallow, slow stroke to stay in place beside the dock.

"I do!" Amelina shouted back, glad he didn't want tobacco or indigo. Nonc Alain had let the fields farther back from the bayou go without planting this year and she herself had managed only the high garden on the levee top and the cotton patch behind the house—less than two arpents of planted ground.

"If you will wait just a moment!" she called and held still, watching for the man's reaction.

He nodded. Then he lifted his oars again and maneuvered his bateau closer to the big cypress pylons that held the planked dock above the water. "I will wait. I have all day to visit these others." He pointed down the bayou, gesturing at the houses dotted along the banks on either side.

Amelina turned and ran back inside, holding her bonnet in place with one hand as she reached upward with the other to take the egg basket from its hook. The cypress handle fit into her palm perfectly. Nonc Alain had replaced the old palmetto handle, so frayed it had finally given way. This was the third handle for the egg basket, he had told Amelina. He had made it for Magarite, his youngest sister.

Amelina sighed. Magarite Fotentot was thirty now, with seven children of her own, living down the bayou just a little ways. Amelina could see her fine big house from the top of the levee. Anne and Sally slept in the downstairs room adjacent to their parents' boudoir. Sometimes Amelina wished she had gone there when her parents had died; it would have been like having two sisters. She would have had someone to whisper secrets to at night.

But, she reminded herself, it would also have meant having five ornery brothers. The boys slept in the *garçonerrie*, up the steep outside stairs, but all day long they plagued Sally and Anne, playing tricks and teasing. If the Fotentots had had more room, Amelina thought, I would have ended up there, not here. She sighed again.

"Perhaps I shall go spend the day with Sally and Anne tomorrow," Amelina said aloud as she danced down the back steps. Running across the sunlit yard, she dodged around the *cuisine*—the little kitchen shed was barely used when Nonc Alain was gone. Amelina usually cooked a stew on Saturdays that lasted her all week. Sometimes she paddled across the bayou and joined Tante Rosemarie's family for supper.

Just beyond the kitchen shack, Amelina had to skirt Nonc Alain's slow-growing pile of winter stove wood. The ax was wedged into the chopping block. Split pieces of cypress and oak littered the ground.

Even this early, the sun was warm on Amelina's shoulders and back as she turned to untie the leather latch on the chicken coop door. Within, she could hear Vagabond fussing at his hens. He always acted as though it was their fault his crowing did not open the door each morning.

The big rooster's impatience was unfair, especially since it was he himself who caused the chickens to be locked in much of the time. That was why Nonc Alain had named him Vagabond; he wandered far and wide if allowed to. And he took his hens with him, endangering them all—especially the four remaining chicks from a late-season clutch. The fluffy yellow babies trailed behind their mother. They were the last batch this year, probably. She had lost five of them since they had hatched.

Amelina pulled the door open. "Come then," she scolded Vagabond. Then she smiled as he clucked anxiously, rounding up his hens, hurrying them outside. He strutted in half circles, then stretched up to crow once more.

"The sun knows it is to rise, silly rooster," Amelina teased. Then she shook her head. Talking to the chickens!

Amelina pushed her hands into the corn husks that lined the nests, feeling for eggs. She found eleven eggs. Three were still warm. She laid them all carefully into the basket, then turned to go out. She left the door standing open.

"Don't you go too far," she called to Vagabond.

The big rooster was scratching at the soil, making the short, sharp clucking sounds that told his hens he had found something good for them to eat.

Halfway across the yard, Amelina heard a raucous cry and looked back. Crows. Were they getting the chicks? Amelina glanced up at the enormous old oak tree that shaded the back half of the yard. She had been watching, but so far she had not seen the *poulette* thief.

Amelina glared at the tree. She did not like crows. They were too sly. She squinted, unable to see any of the big blue-black birds, even though she had heard the cawing clearly.

She knew they were perched somewhere in the dense branches, just waiting for a chance to swoop down. Amelina set down the eggs and grabbed up three slim pieces of the kindling. Shouting, she flung the wood at the oak tree, sending Vagabond and his hens scuttling across the dusty yard.

Three crows appeared, startled into flight, and Amelina shook her fist at them as they rose higher and turned, sliding over the crown of the oak to disappear from sight.

Amelina picked up the basket, wishing Nonc Alain were here this morning, where he should be, not away from his *maison*, his home. One person was not enough to tend to everything that needed care on this farm. The pure-blooded sow was close to birthing, and the weeds in the corn patch by the high garden were getting thick again.

Amelina pushed a strand of hair back beneath her bonnet and straightened her dress, then picked up the egg basket. Whatever her uncle was up to in his constant traveling, he needed to spend more time here, on his farm.

Amelina went out the front door and walked up the slope toward the bayou. Topping the levee, she studied the *marchand*. He was neither old nor young. His face was kind enough, and he was waiting patiently, his eyes half closed as he enjoyed the earliest sun of the day. He had brought his bateau right up behind her little pirogue and had aligned it next to the dock. When he saw her coming, he smiled. "Bonjour," he called out again in his awkward French. Then he added the words, "Good morning!"

"Hello!" Amelina called back in English, and his smile widened.

CHAPTER TWO

"You speak English?" the marchand called out and the eagerness in his voice was almost comic.

"I do," Amelina assured him.

"The buttons are for yourself?" the marchand asked as she stepped onto the planked dock and carried the basket toward him. She had piled it high with the new eggs, and nearly twenty more from the cool box in the cuisine.

"*Non,*" Amelina said automatically, then switched back to English. "For my uncle's new jacket."

"And you have made it for him?"

Amelina blushed and nodded. His admiring tone made it seem likely that he appreciated the time and effort in weaving cloth and sewing. Few men truly did. Still smiling at her, he reached out for the egg basket, and she handed it to him. While he counted the eggs into a crate that was already half full, she looked off toward the east. The early sun was bright and warm.

"Well, then, which of these do you prefer?" the marchand was saying.

Amelina lowered her eyes. He was holding up several stiff paper cards for her to see. Each one held eight buttons. They were sewn on securely as though the paper were a piece of cloth. Amelina shook her head. "Too small for a jacket."

The marchand nodded pleasantly. "I have more." He stood up and stepped onto the dock, reaching for his mooring rope. He looped the rope through the wooden blocks, tied his bateau, then knelt to pull a box from the stern onto the dock. He lifted the fitted lid and pushed it toward Amelina. She sat carefully, arranging her skirt modestly, then began to go through the buttons. A set of shiny black ones stood out from all the rest. Amelina showed her choice to the marchand.

"A fine eye for quality, young miss."

Amelina blushed again and looked across the bayou. Tante Rosemarie was out in her garden now, but still watching. She waved when she saw Amelina turn toward her. Then she bent back over her okra plants. The nights were cooling now, but it would be a while before the okra and potatoes were finished for the year.

"This is how the sales agents do it up north," the marchand was saying. His face looked earnest, boyish. "I sew them onto the cards myself."

"It looks very nice," Amelina said, almost forgiving him for using her nickname earlier.

"Have you ever been up north?"

The question startled Amelina. She shook her head. "I have never been farther away from here than Vermilionville, and there only twice."

"But your English . . . ?"

Amelina explained about her mother, quickly, and was relieved when he asked her no more.

"I have seen Baltimore and New York City and Philadelphia," the man said.

Amelina shook her head and laughed. "Are the Yankees up north as cold and mean as people say?"

"They didn't seem so to me when I was there," the man said. "Now, I ain't so sure. They've torn the plantations down to the ground on Opelousas Road and all down Bayou Teche."

Amelina narrowed her eyes. "Why?"

The man pulled in a deep breath and let it out. "I don't know, miss. I can't fathom what would make a man think he had the right to do what they're doing."

Amelina shivered in spite of the early sunshine. "I thought they would all go home soon. Are they tearing up Vermilionville?" Amelina asked, pitying the people who lived there and wishing Nonc Alain would never go there again.

"Not so much," the marchand answered. "The

officers held them in there. Or so far, it seems. I just hope our boys can turn them around before they get as far as Texas."

The man had straightened the button cards in the box. He rubbed at his forehead now. "There's a Catholic school up the Opelousas Road, east of the railroad, north of Grand Coteau . . . "

"Sacred Heart Convent?"

The man looked up. "You know it?"

Amelina shrugged. She was not about to explain to a stranger that she was arguing with her uncle and a priest about her future at that very same convent. He would certainly never guess it. The girls who went to the convent academy came from wealthy families for the most part. Nonc Alain had said there were more students now because their parents were pretty sure even the Yankees would not be low enough to ruin a nuns' school.

The marchand frowned. "They say the Yankees even visited there, but that they did no harm."

"But Vermilionville is all right?" Amelina asked.

"Is that where your uncle has gone to?" The marchand asked. "Your aunt said he was off somewhere."

Amelina frowned. She looked across the water to see Tante Rosemarie still watching, glancing up as she went about her work. She would keep an eye on things until the marchand was gone. Not that he was likely any danger at all.

The river peddlers were mostly honest men, Amelina knew. How could they be otherwise here on the bayous? One shout would bring help on the run and a gunshot would bring every man in hearing distance.

"Folks who opposed the war are finding an interest now," the marchand was saying. "Because of the behavior of the Yankees." The man nodded, as though he was agreeing with himself. "They fought a battle two days ago up near the Chertiens' plantation. And they broke up Miss Mouton's funeral."

Amelina felt a chill go through her. The Moutons were famous, well known to everyone in Louisiana—not just the Cajuns. Jean Jaques Mouton was a brigadier general in the Confederate army. Old man Mouton and his wife had founded Vermilionville.

"Cecilia Mouton died," the marchand was saying. "Some Yankee went up on the church roof and was waving torches around—Yankee signaling of some kind, I suppose. There was a tale going around that another soldier took the box of funeral candles and was going to walk right off with it until an officer stopped him."

The marchand shook his head as he lifted his oars and took a careful backstroke that brought him back alongside the dock. "They say this General Ord is trying to get the troops to behave like men. But they've already tore down the fences all the way up the road. Burning the cypress rails for their cookfires, then stealing the food to cook. Yankees!" He spat the word out. "If I got a chance, I'd shoot 'em all, one at a time."

Amelina didn't answer. She hated the war. And it was coming so close, right into her own bayou country, to her home. It made her feel sick and uneasy to think of soldiers interrupting people's funerals, stealing and looting crops.

"They are swarming like flies over a carcass," the marchand said, echoing her thoughts.

Amelina stared out over the dark water, the box of buttons forgotten before her. "Who is winning the war? Are the Yankees?"

The marchand shrugged. "Depends on who you talk to. The Confederates, from what I've heard."

"Will the Yankees stay in Vermilionville?" Amelina wondered aloud, not really expecting him to answer.

"If our boys can't stop them, they'll go up to Opelousas," the man said. "Then on to the Sabine. At least folks are saying they are Texas bound. Like a swarm of blue flies." He gestured at the bayou. "There's enough of them to choke your little bayou for miles. Enough to clean out your chicken coop and your corrals and tramp down your garden and be gone all before dinnertime." He turned and spat into the brownish water.

He slung one box, then another, onto the planks. Amelina glanced at the sun. Perrine would end up waiting, but she would understand when Amelina explained to her that a marchand had come. Everyone missed the marchands since the war had begun. Amelina frowned. The war had changed everything.

"You don't have salt to trade, do you?" the man asked suddenly.

Amelina shook her head. "No one does. Not since the Yankees came. Nonc Alain says they have no right to—"

"Everyone says it," the marchand interrupted her. "And still, every pound of salt that comes out of the Avery Island mines is used to salt Yankee pork now. It's getting so no one has enough even for their own meat. If you can get hold of salt, I'd trade fair for it. That's a nice old pirogue," he said suddenly, and Amelina looked at her little boat.

"My father made it."

The marchand nodded appreciatively. "He was a skilled man."

Amelina nodded.

"Here, now look at these." The marchand began laying out his goods. The button boxes were clever, with hinges that opened at an angle, holding a slanting stack of trays open so she could peer in. He had dyed cotton thread and hooks and eyes and all manner of findings for sewing. Amelina hung onto the black buttons, then chose a card of plain hooks and eyes. She would soon be making herself another dress. And this time, Tante Honorine had promised, she would dye the cloth for it. She had indigo to spare this year, she had said. "Did I have enough eggs for both of these?" Amelina asked, hoping the man was honest. She really had no idea what the black buttons were worth now that things were so hard to come by. The hook-and-eye sets were probably not worth more than a few eggs.

The man nodded. "And a little more. I have some fine-point steel needles. No more are coming in from France now that the Yankees have—"

"I have needles," Amelina interrupted him, to stop his war talk before he could get started again. As curious as she was, it made her stomach queasy to think about so many soldiers being so close. "I want these, too." She showed him the hooks and eyes.

The man nodded knowingly. "Making yourself a new waist?" He eyed her plain brownish cotton dress and Amelina found herself blushing again. Most of the other girls and women wore colorful dresses every day, not just to church. They grew a little indigo to make blue dye, or dug roots to make reds and yellows. But most of them lived in households with many pairs of hands to share the work. It was harder for her.

"You weave well," the marchand was saying.

Amelina nodded and thanked him politely for

the compliment. It was true. Her spinning and weaving were better than most girls her age—better than some of the grown women. Her threads were even, her finished cloth flat and smooth. Nonc Alain was a fine weaver. He had taught her.

"Just the buttons and the hooks then?" the marchand asked, and Amelina heard an impatient tone creeping into his voice. She didn't blame him. He had spent a long time talking to a girl who only wanted two small items.

The man cleared his throat. "Is there something else you want?"

Amelina nodded. "May I have a length of ribbon long enough to decorate a bonnet?"

"I only have a few left," the marchand told her as he set another box on the dock. As he opened it, she could see there were only a dozen or so spools of laces and ribbons inside. As she looked closer, she saw that most of them were dirty or worn.

"The dark blue," Amelina said. The card it was wound on looked soiled on the edges, but the ribbon was unspoiled. She reached in and fished it out of the box, then glanced up in time to catch an odd worried look on the face of the marchand.

"Did you hear that?"

She shook her head. "What was it?"

"Gunfire, maybe," he said quietly, then stood and turned to face west. Amelina straightened, holding the ribbon card, breathing through her parted lips, listening. For a long moment she heard nothing. Then, barely audible, there was a single gunshot. When a long silence followed it, she smiled.

"That's nothing."

The marchand nodded. "Sounds like someone hunting, or someone's wife just had a girl baby," the marchand said, relief obvious in his voice. But the instant he finished speaking, there were more shots, tiny, distant popping sounds.

Amelina held very still. Months before, in the spring, she had heard shots like this, barely audible, somewhere to the south. The war had come no closer then, but perhaps this time, it would. She looked across the bayou and saw Tante Rosemarie standing faced away from her, looking in the direction of the gunfire.

"You can just take that whole card," the marchand said as he bent to close up his boxes.

Amelina thanked him absently, and he responded without looking at her as he set the boxes in his bateau, then untied the mooring line. He got in and picked up his oars.

"Will the war come here?" Amelina breathed, knowing he couldn't hear her. He set off, heading downstream.

CHAPTER THREE

Amelina stood uneasily on the dock, shifting her weight, the cypress planks still nighttime cool against the soles of her feet. She listened until the sounds of the distant gunfire stopped. Then she stood a little longer as the marchand rowed out of sight, following the bend of the bayou where the trees hung out over the water.

The silence continued, marred only by the sudden rasping call of a crow. Others joined in, setting up a racket Amelina knew all too well. She scooped up her empty egg basket and turned toward the house, gathering up her skirt to run down the dock. She jumped far enough to clear the muddy place near the last planks, pounding up the gentle rise to the top of the natural levee, then back down, following the house path.

Amelina flung open the wide front door into the salon and ran straight through the house, tossing the basket along with the buttons and ribbon onto the old pink settee Nonc Alain had inherited from his mother. Without pausing, Amelina opened the back door and pounded across the *galerie*, then down the steps into the bright sunlight again.

There, not far from the trunk of the oak tree, she saw four crows on the ground, all of them facing a hen. Her feathers were puffed up, her tail stiff and upright as she crouched over her chicks.

Amelina shouted and clapped her hands. The crows took flight, but slowly, and then circled away in long, lazy curves. They were not afraid of her, Amelina knew. They were clever enough to see she carried no gun. They would only wait until she was gone, then they would be back. Once crows started killing the little puffed yellow poulettes, it was hard to stop them. Amelina frowned. If Nonc Alain were home, he would have shot at the crows. But his gun was with him—wherever he was.

Amelina shook a fist in the direction the crows had gone. Then she spread her skirt wide, shaking the cloth as she circled the stiff-feathered hen, getting around behind her.

"Go then," Amelina said. "Back inside."

The hen moved reluctantly, exposing her chicks as she stepped away. They remained still for a few seconds, then realized their mother no longer stood between them and the dangerous blue sky. They peeped and scrambled to follow.

Amelina shooed them all the way across the yard, even though Vagabond came from behind the cotton patch to peck at her bare heels, angry at her for frightening his hen.

"You silly fool," Amelina scolded. "You let the crows snatch your chicks away, but you attack me?"

The rooster dodged as she flapped her skirt at him. The hen kept going, almost as though she realized that the only safe place for her brood was in the coop. Amelina scattered a little rice and a handful of cracked corn for the chicks to eat, then went out, shutting the coop door behind her. Vagabond had disappeared, but Amelina could hear him on the other side of the cotton patch, clucking and fussing at the rest of the hens.

Amelina glanced up at the sun once more, looking across the yard, past the cotton patch. The last of the late-ripening bolls were still clinging to the stalks, ruined now by rain and weather. She had meant to pick them.

Walking toward the house, Amelina found herself listening without meaning to. It made her angry. She flew through the rest of her early morning chores. The cow stood patiently to be milked, the pigs gathered around the big trough as she emptied half the cow's milk into it, then added sweet potatoes and corn.

In the smaller pen, the big pink-skinned *truie*

was lying down, her eyes closed. Amelina nudged her gently until she got up and walked around a little and tossed her head. Then she grunted and gathered enough energy to chase Amelina back over the fence.

The sow was within a few days of having her piglets, Amelina was sure. Nonc Alain called the fancy-bred sow Vermine because she had a knack for digging her way out of her pen and causing trouble in the barnyard like any other varmint.

"You won't cause trouble today, will you?" Amelina asked the sow. "You are too big to move! Poor thing. But soon you will have your piglets for company." The sow grunted as Amelina picked up the half-full bucket of milk.

Back in the cuisine, Amelina strained the milk through soft cloth to get out the flecks of hay and barnyard grit, then set the big glass bowl down into the cooling basin. The water inside rose as the bowl settled into place. Amelina covered it with another scrap of clean cloth to keep out the flies, then she washed her hands in the tin tub, using only a single dipperful of water to get the soap off. There had been little rain so far this fall. They had to make the water in the cistern do for a while.

Amelina rinsed the milk bucket and hung it upside down to dry, then took down a basket. She wrapped a slab of cold boiled pork in a clean cloth and set it in the bottom, then wrapped some of the corn bread she had baked a few days before. Perrine would enjoy it, she was sure. Perrine's family had many hands to help with work, but also many mouths to feed. Corn bread would be a luxury for her on this ordinary day.

Amelina turned to the hearth, wishing she had had time the day before to boil some corn for fried *couche-couche*—that was Perrine's favorite. Sighing, Amelina filled a water bottle and corked it. Then, she peered into the big kettle at this week's stew. There was still more than enough to last through Friday.

As Amelina went out the door, she latched it shut. The latch would not keep out human thieves, should the Yankees decide to come through the swamps after all, but it would keep out a wild dog, or a nosy possum—far more likely visitors, Amelina hoped.

Stepping from the bright sun up onto the wide shaded porch, she stopped and listened again before she opened the door and went in. It was still silent, only the usual sounds of little children's voices from her cousin Joseph's house a little farther up the bayou, the steady chipping of Tante Rosemarie's long-handled *pioche* as she hoed the weeds from around her okra plants.

Inside the house, Amelina checked the hearth to be sure that no hot coals from last night's fire were exposed. Then she secured the doors that led from her room and the salon to the outdoors. Last, she latched the shutters down tight in case it rained before she got back. It would make the house murderously hot to close it up like this—and she didn't always do it when she was leaving for only a few hours. But the sound of the distant battle—if that's what the gunfire had been—had made her feel odd about leaving things open as she usually did. It had made her feel odd about everything.

The sun was hot on Amelina's shoulders as she walked out onto the dock, glancing back twice, wondering if there was anything she had forgotten to do. She set her meal basket into the stern of her pirogue, then loaded her moss-picking pole, careful to turn the spiked end toward the bow where she wouldn't have to worry about stepping on it. Ready at last, she untied the mooring rope. After a few seconds listening to the peaceful silence that came from the west now, she took in a deep breath.

"I am late," Amelina said to herself as she sat on the edge of the dock, using her outstretched toes to pull the little pirogue closer. She stepped into it, graceful and quick to shift her weight to keep it from tipping. She sat carefully on the narrow bench.

A sudden grating cry overhead made Amelina pause long enough to shake her fist at three crows that sailed across the bayou, sliding close to the trees on the other side. Then she picked up the oar her father had carved and listened once more.

The paddle felt friendly and familiar in Amelina's hands as it always did, and she relaxed a little as she dipped it into the dark water and maneuvered backward, away from the dock. Turning her pirogue in a tight circle, taking short, deep strokes on the right, Amelina got it headed upstream. Then she started paddling in an easy rhythm.

As she passed Tante Rosemarie's house, Amelina paddled close to the edge, just skirting the hard-bladed grasses that marked the shallows. But Tante Rosemarie had gone inside and there was no one to wave to.

Across the bayou, Cousin Joseph's little children were playing with sticks, running back and forth, shouting and shrieking. Amelina lifted her hand to greet them, but none of them noticed her gliding past the stand of willows that fronted their farm.

Her cousin Joseph was out working on his levee, and she smiled as he called out a greeting, shading his eyes to see what she had loaded in the pirogue. "Off to gather moss?"

Amelina nodded, pausing in her paddling, dragging the oar in the water to slow the pirogue. "You are going to turn into a boy, Amelina," Joseph teased.

She blushed and he relented. "You are far too pretty to ever be taken for a boy. But where is that uncle of ours today? Isn't he going to help you?"

Amelina ignored his question and smiled at him

as she answered. "I have half the loft full now. When the Yankees leave and the bed makers come back looking for moss for their mattresses—"

"Or, you could tell Alain to bring it all to our *coup du main*," he said, his eyes twinkling. "Everyone will have to bring something, after all."

"When?" Amelina asked.

"I hope in the next week or two," Joseph answered. "I am adding two cabinets to the back galerie. The girls need another bedroom and Isabelle needs a room to work her cotton and set her loom now."

Amelina nodded. Joseph would need a lot of help to gather moss to make the pit full of muddy *bousillage* he would need to fill the walls of his enlarged house. The coup du main would bring dozens of people to work, to share the big supper after the job was done. There would be plenty of hands to shred the moss and feet to trample it into the clay and mud mixture. But if she could bring moss, it would make her feel better about Nonc Alain not being here to join in—and he probably wouldn't be.

"I will see that we bring plenty of moss," she promised. Or I will, she finished, in her thoughts. Joseph didn't know Nonc Alain was gone again—no one did unless someone asked her directly. She had stopped telling people how often she was on her own.

Back paddling to straighten her pirogue, then

nosing it around into the sluggish current, Amelina glimpsed Cousin Joseph's wife, bent over her flower beds. Isabelle was a treasure, that one, even though her family was not of Acadian heritage. She was kind and good and loved Joseph with a fierceness other men envied.

A sharp cracking sound startled Amelina and she jerked around to see one of Joseph's pigs, loose and foraging along the bayou. Fallen branches were snapping beneath its heavy tread. Amelina stared at it, feeling the rapid thudding of her own heart. For an instant, the wood snapping had sounded like gunfire.

CHAPTER FOUR

Settling into a rhythm of paddling that required no more thought than walking did, Amelina steered her pirogue around a half-submerged fallen tree in front of the farm next door. Where the water cleared and deepened, she paddled faster, rounding the first big bend.

Houses faced the water all along this stretch of the bayou. Since every family's land had been split the French way—equally among its children—many of the farms were about the same size, so the houses were like beads on a necklace, spaced evenly along the banks.

"Bonjour," Tante Edna called from her corn patch.

"Bonjour," Amelina called back, slowing a little to look at the corn. Tante Edna was walking the first row, feeling the corn ears as she went. The stalks were all yellowed now, the last of the corn long gone—except for the ears left for next year's seed. Amelina could see the basket sitting on the ground not far from where Tante Edna was standing. Her two youngest children played in the rows, dodging and laughing as they tried to catch each other.

It was time to gather in her own seed corn, Amelina reminded herself. It was one more chore she hadn't gotten around to doing yet. She promised not to let it go much longer. An early freeze would ruin it, then she would have to borrow for next year's planting.

At the next house, no one was outside in the front yard. Amelina knew why. The Guidry family had more work in the fall than most. Monsieur Guidry was a blacksmith, and his wife mended harnesses and restuffed old horse and mule collars with moss. Every year about this time, they would be absent from most of the everyday *vielles* and even the fall *boucheries*, too busy to leave their farm. But the prairie families who brought them their broken harnesses and tools paid them in late calves—usually more than they could use. So later in the year, when they could come, they often brought more than their share of the meat to any winter gatherings—especially weddings or funerals.

As she paddled on, the dark water dripping from her oar, Amelina nodded greetings to people she had known all of her life. Her cousins and second cousins glanced at her and she could tell some of them had wistful looks on their faces as they watched her pass.

Amelina knew why. With Nonc Alain gone so much of the time, she was on her own more than any of them—even the boys. She came and went as she pleased. Amelina smiled and tried to look like she was worthy of envy—even though she knew she was not.

She didn't cry about her parents too much anymore—but she missed them terribly. It was awful not to have anyone care if she left the farm—and no one to get angry if she was late coming back.

Amelina knew that after her parents had died of the fever, all the relatives had been willing to take her in, but Nonc Alain had been the one who needed a companion the most. His own wife had been lost in childbirth, along with their child, and his sorrow, his *gros deuil*, had kept him from remarrying. And so it had been decided that he would take over Amelina's care and that she would live on his farm, helping him the way she would help her own parents. It was also assumed she would become his heir . . . that his farm would one day be hers.

Nonc Alain's farm was ten arpents—one third of his father's original farm. That meant it was bigger than many of the places along the bayou, but he used very little of the land. He liked hunting much more than he liked plowing. Amelina hoped to find a husband who liked to farm like her Nonc Jean across the bayou. He was almost always home with Tante Rosemarie and their children.

As she let her thoughts wander, Amelina followed the bends in the bayou, sometimes taking one side, sometimes the other. Where it widened out and the cypress grew thick, she followed paths she knew well. Once she heard an alligator slide into the water, but the unmistakable sluicing sound came from a narrow slough that branched off to the west.

Coming around a stand of willow that hung out over the water, Amelina came into a place where the bayou widened and cypress trees grew in a scattered pattern. She knew her way through this little marsh and she paddled without stopping or even pausing. Her pirogue slid steadily through the water, pushing the spears of grass aside as she turned to the left at just the right moment. Then she came back on an angling course, avoiding the worst of the snags: a fallen cypress that lay a hand's span or so underwater. Its branches were a trap for any boat that tried to pass that way.

As Amelina cleared the last bend, she saw Perrine sitting on the dock, carding cotton. The sun haloed her bonnet and lit the bright stripes of her dress. Tante Honorine, Perrine's mother, was an expert weaver and dyer. Perrine herself was getting very good at it. Amelina glanced down at her own plain dress. She really did need to learn to dye. Maybe, when Nonc Alain came back, he could watch over the place and feed the stock while she stayed here a few days with Tante Honorine.

"I didn't mean to be so late," Amelina called when Perrine looked up and met her eyes across the water.

Perrine set her baskets aside and stood up quickly. "Is anything wrong?"

"No," Amelina answered, "but I heard gunshots!" She paddled closer, pushing hard to make the pirogue glide through the dark water.

Perrine's mouth opened as if she were about to speak, but she said nothing for a few seconds. "Soldiers, you mean?"

Amelina nodded and let the pirogue bump gently into the side of the dock.

Perrine pushed her bonnet back. "We didn't hear anything here."

"It was somewhere west of us."

"Is Nonc Alain gone now?" Perrine asked.

Amelina nodded and gave her usual answer. "Down to Vermilionville, he said. Supposed to be back soon."

Perrine smiled, tucking a strand of long dark hair back beneath her bonnet. "I would be afraid in a house all by myself."

Amelina shrugged. "I am used to it, I suppose." She took in a breath, wanting to tell Perrine about the marchand, to ask if he had stopped here, too. But before she could say anything more, Perrine shuddered theatrically.

"I would be afraid. I don't think I could stand waking up in an empty house. But you manage, don't you?" She bent to pick up her baskets, shaking her head and smiling as though they were talking about whether or not Amelina liked crawfish bellies, or about how she preferred peppers in her rice.

But it wasn't a little thing like that, Amelina thought, her cheeks flushing. She hated it. It wasn't as if she *wanted* to wake up in a silent house every morning. Or that she liked being alone a lot of the time. Amelina felt her eyes flooding, but Perrine didn't notice. She was gathering up stray tufts of cotton from the dock planks.

Then, as Amelina fought her tears, Perrine straightened, the basket of clean white cotton dangling from her right hand, the basket full of uncarded cotton, speckled with seeds and dirt, in her left.

At that moment, one of Perrine's sisters appeared at the top of the levee.

"Papa says you have to let me use your hairbrush," she shouted.

Perrine made a comical face, looking back at Amelina. "Perhaps you are the lucky one, after all!" She grinned and started toward her house. "Let me just put these inside and then I am ready," she called back over her shoulder. Her voice was warm and light. She was laughing.

Amelina felt a quick swell of anger. Perrine was

making it sound as though she was fortunate to be an orphan, to live with an uncle who didn't seem to want a daughter, not really.

"It was hardly my choice," she said, and saw Perrine turn, startled. "Do you think I want to live alone?" Amelina went on, unable to keep her anger out of her voice.

Amelina heard the shrillness in her voice, and knew it was unfair, but she couldn't seem to control it. She watched as Perrine's startled look darkened into a frown. Amelina tried to think of something to say that would soften her outburst, but she couldn't.

"I didn't mean—" Perrine began.

Amelina scuffed her foot along the dock, ignoring the prickle of the rough wood planks. She stared at her brown, calloused feet and felt tears sting her eyes again. "Lucky," she said, just loudly enough for Perrine to hear her. "Lucky that my parents died. That I have no brothers or sisters."

Perrine's frown deepened. "I only meant—"

"You meant you couldn't stand it, but since it is me, not you, it is a joke." Amelina interrupted her.

"I meant that it must be difficult and that you—"

"I think I will go home now," Amelina burst out. "I prefer to be alone, as you know."

"Amelina, please!" Perrine shook her head. "You are being unfair with me."

"You think only of yourself!" Amelina shouted at her.

"That is a lie," Perrine shouted back. It was clear that she was angry now, too.

Amelina opened her mouth to speak, but nothing would come out. Perrine just stared at her in silence for another moment, then whirled and ran up over the top of the levee and disappeared from sight.

Amelina tossed her mooring rope back into the pirogue and got in, pushing off the dock with her paddle. She turned the little boat toward home and leaned hard into her paddle strokes, refusing to look back in case Perrine had climbed the levee to watch her.

Pushing her oar deep and bending her back, Amelina made the pirogue fly over the water. She would not go home. There was no real reason not to go moss picking alone as long as she was careful. And if she was late in getting back, who would care?

As she paddled, her face wet with tears, Amelina tried to figure out what had happened. Perrine was her cousin and her friend—her best friend. Their birthdays fell within a few months of each other, and they had been friends as long as Amelina could remember.

Amelina cut the water with smooth, fierce strokes of the paddle. She skirted a stand of live oak trees that grew on a low point close to the edge of the bayou. Only in their highest branches could she see long silvery strands of Spanish moss. This close to people's farms, the moss was picked often. She was going to have to go a fair distance alone—which made her feel angry all over again. Perhaps she should go home after all.

Amelina bit at her lip, knowing she wasn't nearly as upset with Perrine as she was with herself. The truth was she was probably jealous of Perrine—of her big, cheerful family and her parents, Tante Honorine and Nonc George. They were both loud talkers, and they laughed a lot and told stories. Nonc George's stories were always funny.

"I am foolish," she said aloud. "I have insulted my best friend."

The pirogue was fairly flying now as she paddled hard, reaching with every stroke, dragging the oar back through the water with the paddle face flat. The slow current was in her favor now as she tried to leave her·unhappy thoughts behind. She knew that if she looked up, people would wave or call her name as she went by, but she didn't want to talk to anyone.

Amelina gritted her teeth and blinked her stinging eyes. It made no sense. She was lonely and tired of being alone, yet she wanted to avoid anyone who might want to talk to her.

She maneuvered past the fallen cypress again, then hurried on. Coming around the last curve of the bayou before the home place, she slowed, breathing hard, letting the pirogue glide. Joseph had gone in, or was working somewhere behind his house, and she was relieved not to have to explain what had happened. Tante Rosemarie was invisible behind her high levee now and Amelina was glad.

As she paddled in close to the dock, Amelina felt the stinging behind her eyes begin again and she finally let herself cry, sitting up straight in her pirogue, her back to anyone who might see her. She let the hot tears run down her cheeks, careful not to make very much noise.

Crying first about Perrine's unkindness, then her own unfairness—Amelina soon found herself crying about her parents and then, at last, about Nonc Alain and his mysterious trips. It was bad enough to live alone; it was even worse to live with someone she could not quite trust. He was foolish in his ways sometimes—not like a real father should be. He loved her and he took care of her, but he also gambled too often and sometimes got into fights at a *fais do-do* when all the other men his age had put their children to sleep in the back room so they could dance with their wives.

"He is like a boy who has gotten old," she said aloud. "But it is not his fault his wife died when they were both so young," Amelina added, then realized how much she had talked to herself that morning and felt her cheeks flush. She sounded like some old woman. Being alone was making her silly and muddled.

Amelina stood up and stepped onto the dock,

bending to pick up her mooring rope as she did so. She tied her pirogue securely and then stood looking downstream.

She would say something to Nonc Alain, she promised herself. Even if it made him angry. She could imagine him drawing himself up straighter, his boots solid and heavy on the planked floor, telling her a wife might have the right to speak to him so, but not a daughter.

"And I am not really your daughter," Amelina murmured to his image. And she saw, in her imagination, how saying such a thing would hurt his pride—and his feelings.

Amelina shook her head. She did envy Perrine and Sally and Anne and every other girl she knew. Life was simple for them. Perrine didn't have to worry about Tante Honorine and Nonc George. They were the ones to worry about her.

"I will go pick moss tomorrow," Amelina whispered. She gathered up her food basket and picking pole and forced herself to walk up the dock, jumping to clear the mud puddle at the end. Then she trudged up the levee. At the top she stopped and stood, staring down at the planked building with its wide doors and the long galerie that ran across the front, like a visor on a hat.

Amelina tried to take another step, but found she couldn't. She just stood in the hot midmorning sunlight, her basket in one hand and her pole in the other. Then she turned and very deliberately started back toward her boat.

She did not want to go into the empty, silent house. If she was going to spend the day by herself, in silence, she would do it in the swamp, gathering moss. Then at least she would have something to show for this unhappy, lonely day.

CHAPTER FIVE

Amelina paddled downstream instead of upstream—
she didn't want to pass Perrine's dock until she knew
she would not get upset again. It was hardly Perrine's
fault she had lost her parents. It wasn't anyone's fault.

The pirogue slipped through the water as she
passed from the bright October sunshine into the
shade of a row of enormous old magnolia trees
along the front of the La Fleur place. They had been
planted by old man La Fleur's great-grandfather when
he had first settled the place. Amelina had heard the
story a dozen times. The old man had been deported
from Nova Scotia with the rest of the Acadians. He
had lived through the terrible journey in the hold of
the ship, but then he had been sold into slavery up
north. It had taken him fifteen years to work his way
to freedom and come south. Amelina's own great-
grandfather had a similar story. But he had returned
to France for a decade before coming to Louisiana. It
was a common enough story. Most of the Acadian

families had tales every bit as sad. Almost all the people who had been forced to leave Nova Scotia had been scattered, and many had died.

Amelina looked up at the trees. They were close to a hundred years old, she knew. They had grown into each other—a tangle of massive limbs. When they bloomed it was a sight and scent from heaven.

The sun on the water seemed too bright as the pirogue came out of the shade. A sudden soft splash up ahead made Amelina hesitate midstroke. She slowed the pirogue until she could spot the big alligator scrambling up the far bank. There was a well-worn slide, a bare path through the grass. That meant the 'gator lived here. This was its stretch of the bayou, its home.

Amelina steered the pirogue to the other side, keeping a watchful eye on the retreating animal until only the swaying of the willow thicket told her it had kept going. Most 'gators didn't mind if you passed through their homes so long as you didn't bother them further.

On a long straightaway, Amelina noticed a stand of live oaks a little ways back from the bayou. There was no moss on them at all. She lifted her oar from the water and laid it across her lap. If the live oaks had no moss, none of the other trees would.

Amelina sat still for a moment, letting the boat drift, trying to decide where to go for moss. She had to respect the rights of the farmers. On a normal day, with a companion, it wouldn't frighten her at all to go much farther from home. But this was not a normal day—and the sound of gunfire that morning had unnerved her. "I should have gone upstream," she said aloud, then flushed again. Talking to herself had really become a habit.

She let the slow current carry the pirogue forward as she sat, trying to decide what to do. She had wasted a lot of the morning rowing back and forth. If she had stayed home, she would have at least gotten some of her chores done.

"But I wanted to spend a day with Perrine," she reminded herself and didn't bother to blush about talking out loud. Taking a deep breath, she began to paddle again. It was a fine warm morning and the quietness of the water soothed her raw feelings. The rhythm of paddling calmed her heart. The farms slid past slowly but steadily until she was past most of them, headed into country she didn't know very well. When the banks held only scattered houses, Amelina began to scan the countryside carefully as she went.

Then, Amelina noticed a narrow branch of the bayou leading off to the left. She put her paddle back in the water and angled her strokes just enough to nose the pirogue into the still water of the smaller bayou.

Amelina rowed carefully. There were a thousand

places in the swamps where the water became suddenly shallow, tangled with snags and roots that could trap a pirogue. Willow clumps slid past, and a stand of live oaks. Amelina kept her eyes moving as Nonc Alain had taught her. She was constantly scanning the deep grass for signs of a 'gator slide, watching the soft mud for bear tracks, the water's surface for the curving ripple of a snake's passage.

Threading her boat through an especially thick growth of sharp-edged grasses, Amelina saw that the passage narrowed up ahead. She slowed. If the bayou was going to get so close-sided that she wouldn't be able to turn her pirogue around—it was better to go back now. If no one kept this passage clear and she had dead-ended on the narrow point of someone's farm, the owners would probably take a dim view of her foraging for moss on their land. Amelina shaded her eyes and peered ahead. It looked like the passage went through, but she wasn't sure.

Amelina had almost decided to turn around when she spied a stand of big live oaks—draped in thick strands of Spanish moss. She paddled toward them and saw the waterway widen when she came around the next bend. She smiled. At least one thing was going to work out in her favor today.

Amelina paddled a little faster now, looking on either side of the narrow bayou for signs that this was someone else's land. There were none. She saw no footprints, no staked bins to hold picked moss, nothing at all to warn her someone else had the right to it.

Amelina nosed the pirogue into the soft, muddy bank. This was a *coteau*—just the natural high ground that bordered a bayou. No one had built a levee here. It didn't look as though anyone ever came here at all.

Amelina got out, looking up at the trees. She smiled again, imagining how pleased Joseph would be if she brought even half the moss she would be able to gather here to his coup du main. Whistling tunelessly, still smiling, Amelina took her long pole from the pirogue and set to work. She walked around the first oak, looking upward at the curtains of gray green moss.

The strands were thick as any she had ever seen. She reached up to finger the moist, silvery moss. Then she leaned forward to breathe in the soft, musty scent. For the first time since she had left Perrine's, her heart lifted a little.

Reaching upward with the long pole, Amelina tangled the spikes in the moss, then jerked downward. For an instant, nothing happened, but then the strand broke and snaked to the ground. Amelina unwound the ends from her spiked pole, then reached upward again.

In an hour, Amelina had the pirogue full of moss. She had packed the layers as well as she could, stuffing more down the sides, to fill the little spaces where the pirogue curved outward.

Since the mound of moss made the boat a little top heavy, Amelina decided to play it safe and turn the pirogue around by hand. Using the mooring rope and her paddle, she nudged the pirogue's bow away from the coteau with her hand, then pushed at the bow by leaning out with the paddle. The pirogue angled in the water and she drew it forward at the same slant, nosing it into the bank again. Then she repeated the process, this time managing to pull the bow far enough around to step in.

Amelina sat down quickly and was about to lower her oar into the water when she heard something moving in the stiff-bladed grass on the far side of the bayou. She tensed, immediately uneasy, trying to tell if the animal was moving away from her or toward her. In a narrow bayou like this one, an alligator sometimes felt cornered and crowded. If it was a bear, it was probably just loping away but . . .

The oddest sound caught Amelina's attention. It was a low moaning, like a ghost in a story. She held her breath for a second. Maybe someone had shot a bear and it had run off here to die alone. If it was hurt, it would be incredibly dangerous.

Amelina stared at the slope that rose from the water's edge. She couldn't see beyond it. The sound came again, but much softer. This time, it sounded more like a dog. Perhaps someone's hound was hurt. She winced, hoping the animal could make it home if it needed help. She leaned forward, stretching up to see over the top of the mound of moss in the bow.

It was foolish even to go look, Amelina thought. There was nothing she could do for a wounded animal. She had no gun to end its misery, and she could easily get hurt trying to do anything else.

Amelina raised her oar, but then she lowered it again, sitting very still, her paddle ready if something dangerous should come charging over the coteau. Seconds ticked past and the sound didn't come again.

Amelina blinked, narrowing her eyes against the bright sun, her whole body aching from the tenseness of her posture. The grass had stopped rustling. Whatever it was had stopped moving—or had moved on.

Amelina exhaled and put her paddle in the water again. She took a short, slanted stroke to turn the bow, then another to push away from the bank. She was lowering her oar for the third time, when the sound came again. Or at least she thought it did. It was so low she wasn't sure.

"And now you are imagining things!" she whispered to herself.

Then it came once again. It was just as soft, but because Amelina was listening hard, she was sure this time. And it did sound like a dog whimpering, not a bear or anything truly dangerous. Maybe, if someone had just left the dog to die, she could take it home and care for it and keep it. Nonc Alain could hardly object to her having a dog so long as it didn't bother the stock. It would help keep the crows away from the chicks, and it would be company for her.

"Then, I could talk to something besides myself," Amelina whispered, trying to make herself laugh. But it was a sad little joke and she knew it.

The dog groaned again. Determined, Amelina took a single strong stroke and her pirogue glided across the narrow bayou and nosed onto the opposite bank. She used her paddle as a pole in the shallow water and angled her boat so that it lay parallel with the shoreline. Then she stepped out, still holding her paddle. It wasn't much of a weapon, but she had no other.

Taking each step carefully, placing her bare feet silently on the soft earth, she stared up the rise. At the top, she stood, scanning the thick grass that ran back to a scattered stand of willows, and beyond them, a fallen oak that leaned on a sweet gum that grew close to it.

"Here, boy," Amelina said tentatively. Then she cleared her throat. "Come on! Where are you, fella?"

There was no sound.

Amelina took another few steps forward, then caught a glimpse of something she didn't understand at first. It was a mottled blue—not the right color for any animal she knew. Staring, advancing a single step at a time, holding her paddle tightly enough to whiten her knuckles, she topped the rise and started downward.

The odd patch of mottled blue she had seen became clearer and larger as she got closer. Three more steps and she stopped again, afraid and uncertain what to do next.

The blue was the jacket of a Union soldier. He lay face down in the dirt, his canteen cast out to one side, his hat on the ground beside him. He was wounded and had been for a long time. The mottling was his blood, soaked into the cloth and drying in the sun.

CHAPTER SIX

Amelina stood, her breath quick and shallow, trying to figure out what to do. The Yankee was so still that for a long moment she thought he was dead. Then he moved, hunching his back and lifting his head half an inch.

Amelina stepped back, raising the oar in her hands, scared of the Yankee even though he seemed too wounded to harm her. She waited, her heart pumping hard, until he collapsed again.

The soldier made a sound of such misery that Amelina moved a step toward him without thinking, then caught herself. What was she doing helping a Yankee? She should leave him here, now.

Amelina found herself wondering what the Confederates would do with him if they found him. Would they shoot him on the spot? She didn't think so, but it was impossible to tell. The vigilante riders before the war had hung men without much fuss, she knew. Everyone had heard the stories before the war—even though the men tried to keep it among themselves. Were soldiers worse than vigilantes? Or better?

The man groaned again and this time Amelina jumped back, startled. He raised his head. Focusing on her, he tried to say something, but his voice rasped, then stuck. Amelina stood still, trembling. He blinked and tried again.

"Water?"

Amelina spun around and ran back down the slope to her pirogue, her heart pounding. She threw her oar in the pirogue, grabbed her water bottle from the meal basket in the stern, and ran back up the coteau.

"I have water," she said when she saw that his head was still up, his eyes still open. A flash of relief and joy crossed his face, then a grimace of pain hardened his features again.

Amelina extended the bottle in one hand, then lowered it. She was afraid to get close to him. Yankees were unpredictable, Mr. Sawyer had said. There was no telling what they would do and no telling how mean-hearted they could be. Other people said the same.

"I'll just set the water down," she said unevenly in English. "I'll just leave it here and—"

"Help me." The soldier's voice was tight and strained, but there was no mistaking his words this time. "Help me," he began again. Then he cleared his throat, wincing. "Help me . . . sit up."

Amelina hesitated, then took a step toward him, still holding out the bottle. She could see the feverish intensity in his eyes as he stared at it. He was looking at it like a man who could see heaven.

"Can't you sit up?" Amelina asked him, stopping a half step away and looking down at him. The back of his neck was sunburned like a farmer's. She could see how filthy he was—the creases in his skin were dark with dirt. There was sand in his hair.

"No." He let his head sink to the ground again.

There was so little hope in his voice that Amelina's heart ached for him and she laid down the bottle. Kneeling beside him, her hands fluttering over his back, she was unsure what to do next. He needed to drink. But if he couldn't sit up, it seemed impossible.

"Mister?" She plucked at his dirty blue coat.

He groaned.

"Mister? You have to try. I can't help if you don't try."

For a moment he lay still, then another terrible moan escaped his lips, and Amelina sat back on her heels as he jackknifed, curling onto his side. He rocked back and forth. After a moment, Amelina understood what he was trying to do and she slid her hands beneath his shoulder and tried to lift him.

He groaned as he managed to come up into a sitting position, his knees bent almost double.

Amelina flinched at the sound of it, and at the terrible smell of his filthy clothes.

He was not steady, and Amelina had to keep one hand on his shoulder for him to keep from falling over. She extended her other hand backward, fishing for the bottle, leaning against him involuntarily. He groaned, deep in his throat, and she swept her hand back and forth, frantic to find the bottle. When her fingers finally fumbled on it, she dragged it forward and picked it up, sitting back away from the Yankee again, her hands shaking.

After struggling for a few seconds to find a way for him to drink without help, Amelina ended up kneeling beside him, propping him up with her shoulder while she used both hands to pull the cork out of the bottle neck. When she tipped it against his lips, he drank with his eyes closed, swallowing in noisy, painful-sounding gulps. After a few seconds, she lowered the bottle.

"I don't think you should drink it all straight down," Amelina said aloud. "It might make you sick to take it all at once."

The Yankee didn't answer. He looked at her sidelong and she saw there was a bloom of fresh red blood on the front of his jacket. Snake-quick, the Yankee suddenly reached for the bottle with both hands, tearing it from her grasp.

Amelina tried to stop him, but in a split second,

he was raising it, groaning with the pain it cost him. Then he drank as though the world had stopped forever, as though he had forgotten that she—or anything else—existed at all.

When the bottle was more than half empty, the Yankee corked it and slumped against Amelina. She dug her feet into the dirt and pushed her shoulder into his, bracing herself to keep him upright. When he started to lean the other way, his own weight more than he could bear, Amelina got a handful of his uniform coat and pulled him straight again. The Yankee murmured something.

"What?" Amelina asked him.

He pointed at the bottle. "Thank you."

"You're welcome," Amelina said politely.

The distant, eerie howl of a hound sent a shock through the Yankee's body that stiffened his spine. Amelina leaned forward.

"It's just someone hunting," she assured him. "Just somebody's gun dog."

The Yankee shook his head. "They're after me," he managed. His voice was jagged with pain.

Amelina glanced southwest, where the baying had come from. "Was there a battle?"

The soldier shook his head, a slow jerky movement. "I was . . . "

His voice faltered and he heaved in a short breath and tried again. "Reconnaissance."

The long, unfamiliar French word startled her because he had pronounced it perfectly, with no trace of his sharp Yankee accent. She knew what the word meant. He had been sneaking around trying to see where the Confederates were. He was a Yankee spy. Amelina saw him watching her from beneath his brows. "*Espion*," she said in French, then repeated it in English. "Spy."

There was a pleading look in his eyes. "Are you . . . Cajun?" he asked after a moment's silence. The dog's distant bay came again and the soldier's eyes flickered southward, then back to her face. "But you speak English as well as French?"

Amelina nodded. "My mother was English. My father was Cajun." He didn't answer and she felt like he wanted her to say more. "I live with my uncle now and I have a lot of cousins," she added, feeling foolish as soon as she had spoken. Why would this man care about her being an orphan, or anything else about her?

"I envy you." He said it in a whisper.

Amelina struggled with the English word "envy" in her mind. She knew what it meant, but it seemed the wrong word.

"It is better"—he stopped and coughed a little, wincing—"not to fight."

Amelina understood. He was hurt and afraid and the war had caused all of it. Everyone knew the Cajuns mostly shunned the war.

The dog bayed again. It had the aimless sound of a dog that has lost the trail. She turned to look into the soldier's eyes.

"You better . . . leave," he said.

Amelina stood up.

"Careful," the Yankee hissed. He coughed and gestured for Amelina. "Keep down."

Amelina nodded and started toward the rise of the coteau. She had topped it and had taken a step downward toward the bayou before she stopped, torn between her own fear and her sympathy for the hurt Yankee. He was bleeding and scared and alone. And yet, when he knew danger was close, he had thought first of her safety.

The dog howled, a long, frustrated call. It was still pretty far away, but how long would that last? Once it found the Yankee's scent, it would come straight on, leading the Confederates at a run. Amelina shivered. She had heard hounds all her life. She knew the vigilantes and some of the slave owners used them to track people, too. She had never thought much about it before, but it made her sick to think about anyone being run down like a possum or some other varmint. "Sssst!"

Amelina straightened a little to see the Yankee making a feeble shooing motion with his hand. "They'll shoot."

Amelina shook her head. "You can come with me."

He made a hopeless gesture. "I can't walk far." His voice was still rough, but the water had helped a little. She could hear him more clearly now.

"I have my pirogue," she told him.

"A boat?" His eyebrows shot up and for a second his surprise overshadowed the pain in his face.

Amelina nodded.

"And you would . . . you would . . . " He couldn't seem to get the rest of the thought out and Amelina nodded to let him know she had understood.

She came forward, stooping to scoop up the water bottle with one hand. Then she positioned herself beside him again and he put one arm around her shoulders. When he leaned upon her to stagger to his feet she very nearly fell, but she managed to keep her balance, taking a wide stance to steady him.

Every step the Yankee took was torturously, incredibly slow. The dog's minor-key howling seemed to be more to the west than the south now and a little farther away. Maybe the dog had lost the trail altogether. Amelina found herself daring to hope.

It was hardest going downhill toward the pirogue. The Yankee leaned on her so hard that she staggered, walking at a slant to support his weight. Glancing up, she saw that the blood on his jacket front had spread anew. His face was white and he held his mouth tight-lipped and rigid. She tried to hold him upright, imagining the pain he had to be in.

Two steps from the pirogue, the Yankee fell, a slow half turn that ended with his knees buckling beneath him. He sank down, even though Amelina tried to keep him standing—until he was on his knees and she was beside him.

"You better just—" He finished the sentence with a jerking motion of one hand. His skin was so white Amelina wondered if he was dying, right now, here beside her on the soft dirt of the coteau.

"Wait here," she told him, scrambling to her feet. In the distance, the dog bayed and the tone of it had changed. It was no closer, but it had picked up the scent again and was singing the news to the world. Amelina found herself sweating in fear, imagining the Confederates bursting out of the palmetto and grass on the far side of the little bayou and opening fire.

Looking up to scan the southwestern horizon, Amelina tripped but caught herself and kept going. With shaking hands, she gathered up her tie rope and pulled the pirogue a little way up onto the muddy shore. She made herself stop and consider, thinking about the weight of the soldier. If she pulled the pirogue too far up the bank, she wouldn't be able to push it back in the water. If she didn't pull it up far enough, the wounded man would never be able to get into it. And if he fell into the water . . .

Bare feet squishing in the mud, Amelina adjusted the position of her boat, then began to wrestle with the moss. Pulling it out one double armful at a time, she worked hard, running upslope a few steps to drop every load on dry ground. Frantic, dragging in uneven breaths, she emptied the boat. Then, cursing herself for not thinking of it first, she replaced some of the moss, lining the hard planks of the bow.

Running her eyes over the palmettos and trees to the southwest again, she sprinted back to the Yankee. "Hurry," she said, listening for the hound but unable to hear it over the sound of her own breathing.

It took three tries to get the soldier on his feet, and Amelina was frantic as they finally took the first staggering step together. He was desperate not to fall, she could tell, and he used every ounce of strength he had to put one foot in front of the other, one arm around her shoulders and the other extended for balance.

Amelina helped him turn to face the stern, standing alongside the pirogue, bruising her ankle on the planks of the boat. She held his forearm as he managed to step in, then crashed to his knees. The boat tipped as he fell.

"Lie down, lie down!" Amelina pleaded.

He groaned with the effort it took for him to untangle his legs. He lay back slowly at first, his back to the bow, then slumped and fell hard enough to make her wince when he hit his head. The moss dulled the impact, but she heard him groan.

"I'm going to load the moss on top of you," she said, carrying the first armload as she spoke. "I won't cover your face but with a little. The rest I will pile high."

The Yankee said nothing. His eyes were closed. And as Amelina piled the moss back into her little pirogue, she wondered if she was trying to save a man who had already died.

CHAPTER SEVEN

As Amelina ran back and forth to the pile of moss, she fought her fear and kept her eyes on what she was doing. Constantly looking for the Confederates would not help her get away from them. Seeing them coming would do her no good. She had to be back in the water and paddling away before they spotted her at all.

Amelina worked frantically. The moss seemed to tangle and mat, making it hard for her to get the long strands gathered up and back into the boat.

Settling armloads of moss on the Yankee's inert form, Amelina banged her shins on the planks as she leaned over the boat. She worked wads of the moss into the curves of the boat's hull again, packing it as tightly as she could in a wide halo around the Yankee's head, then covering his shoulders and chest. She heard the dog howling twice, but did not look up. Her only chance was to hurry now, to pray that the Confederates would be slow in finding the Yankee's trail—though she knew that because he was bleeding the dogs would be able to follow it easily once they did find it.

The Yankee's eyes were still closed when Amelina laid a thin layer of the moss across his face, then built up the sides of the load a little more. Breathing hard, she stepped back to scan the horizon, then looked back into her boat. The soldier was completely concealed.

Amelina dashed back up the bank and picked up the soldier's canteen and hat. She put them both under the cloth of her meal basket, then ran back to break off two oak boughs. Using them like misshapen brooms, she whirled over the soft dirt, scrubbing out every track she could see. Then she ran for the pirogue, throwing the oak branches across the top of the mound of moss.

Amelina put her oar and her water bottle into the stern of the pirogue, then, flattening her palms against the bow, she shoved hard, breathlessly pushing her little boat back into the dark water.

It wasn't until she was sitting on her narrow bench, using the tip of the paddle to nudge her pirogue straight, she realized she had left deep, scrambling footprints in the mud by the water's edge. Hesitating only a second, she put her oar into the water and pulled hard, bracing her feet on the crosspiece in the hull. The most important thing now was to get away, to put as much distance between where the Confederates thought the Yankee might be and where he actually was.

"Lie still," she said aloud.

There was no movement beneath the moss.

"Lie still no matter what you hear."

"I will," the Yankee said very quietly, and Amelina felt her heart leap. He was alive!

Putting her whole weight behind every stroke, Amelina guided the pirogue up the narrow bayou, listening for the baying of the dog.

She was back past the second bend when she heard the baying again. It was louder and closer, as it had been every time, but now it was coming from behind her. The dogs were following the Yankee's trail to where she had found him. It would take the hunters all of a minute to see that a boat had been pushed up onto the bank, that moss had been gathered in it, that it was being rowed by someone with small, bare feet. But then what would they do? What could they do?

If they were on foot, she had a good chance of making it home without being discovered. If they had boats somewhere—it was going to be much harder to slip past them.

The dog was yowling again and the cries were coming closer together. The bayou narrowed ahead of Amelina and she had to slow down to make it through a set of tortuous, snaky curves, but then it widened and straightened and she rowed hard again, switching her paddle from one side to the other to keep the pirogue straight in the water. The Yankee's weight changed the balance of the boat, slowing her down as she threaded her way through the fallen logs and clumps of willow.

When Amelina felt a dragging thump on the stern her heart paused. Her next oar stroke confirmed her fear. Some snag she hadn't seen had caught the pirogue. She heard the dog yowling, and her heart speeded up. It had changed its tone. It was in full chase now. It had found the scent. Amelina could picture the hound—it would be straining at its leash, dragging its owner along.

Twisting around, trying to spot the submerged log that held her trapped, Amelina slid her feet sideways and forward, accidently bumping the soldier's boots. He groaned.

Amelina winced, turning back. "I'm sorry."

There was no answer, except for the sound of the dog in the distance. Amelina wrenched around again, leaning her weight to the left, then back to the right, rocking the pirogue slightly. She put her oar in the water and shoved backward, timing the stroke to match the pirogue's farthest tilt. Nothing happened. She was still trapped by the snag.

Glancing back over her shoulder at the palmettos

that lined the bayou here, Amelina felt her heart hammering. Rocking back and forth again, violently, tipping the pirogue so far she was afraid it was going to go over, Amelina back paddled again, putting every bit of strength she had into each stroke.

Finally, she felt something grind along the bottom of the boat beneath her bare feet and the pirogue slid backward and floated free.

Her breath ragged and fast, Amelina turned the bow, edging forward again slowly. Alert for even the tiniest drag, easing the pirogue along very slowly, Amelina cleared the snag and let out a long breath of relief. The Yankee's weight made the pirogue ride lower in the water. She would have to be more careful.

Amelina went back to paddling hard, maneuvering the pirogue through the narrow waterway as quickly as she could. Twice more she heard the dog baying, but it sounded farther and farther away. The dog would not be able to follow the Yankee's scent over the water, she knew. So if they didn't get close enough to actually see her in the next few minutes, she could probably make it home safely.

"Are you all right?" she asked aloud as she rounded the curve in the waterway that let her back into the wide and familiar bayou she knew so well. There was no answer. Amelina did not break her rhythm. The important thing now was to hurry. If she could get him home, she would figure out some way to get him inside. Once he was and resting, she would go to Aunt Rosemarie and beg for help. Tante Rosemarie would come, she was sure of it. The trick would be to keep from attracting everyone else's attention. There were some men on the bayou who would never allow a Yankee to stay if they knew he was there. Nonc Jean would not want to draw the Confederates' attention or their anger, she was sure.

Amelina forced her thoughts aside and reached as far as she could with her paddle for every stroke, sinking it deep and pulling hard. Switching sides, she kept the pirogue going straight down the deepest part of the bayou. She braced her feet and let the rhythm of paddling take over and quiet her spinning mind. Her father's paddle seemed part of her hands. The dark brown water slid away beneath the hull of the pirogue. The farms on both sides of the bayou grew closer together again.

"Where are you hurrying off to?"

The voice startled Amelina so badly she fumbled midstroke, very nearly losing her paddle. She recovered her grip in time to see the marchand coming out from behind a dock. He waved and rowed in a curve to head downstream, coming toward her. His bateau was crowded with the boxes and cases that held his wares.

"Is everything all right?" he called as he got closer.

Amelina managed to find her voice. "Fine," she

called back. "Everything . . . is fine." She answered him as calmly as she could, spacing her words between the long breaths she was taking. The pirogue was still sliding forward, but it was slowing now that she held her oar across her lap. She nodded in as friendly a manner as she could manage, then put her paddle back into the dark water. Overhead, a crow shrieked.

"You oughtn't be out and around by yourself like this," the marchand shouted. Amelina's heart sank when she glanced back. He was rowing purposefully now, veering to come alongside. She wanted to scream at him to go away, to leave her alone—but knew she couldn't. Anything she did to make him suspicious would only increase the danger. What had he said? That he wanted to shoot the Yankees one by one?

"I was going to go moss picking with a cousin of mine," Amelina began as he drew near. "But she couldn't go, so I went alone." She tried hard to keep the trembly urgency in her voice from being too obvious. "I was just hurrying on home." She put her oar back in the water as she finished her sentence.

"I have to go back up this way," the marchand said. "I'll just keep close in case any trouble comes along. That was a skirmish we heard this morning."

Amelina felt the cool, slick leather of the Yankee's boot touch her bare toes and she jumped.

She glanced down, then away, just as quickly. The Yankee's boot was covered, but the dark leather was visible if someone looked hard enough.

"You are as nervous as a cat in a thunderstorm," the marchand said. He was grinning.

Amelina smiled, praying the Yankee wouldn't move again or make any noise. The marchand was staring at her. She smiled and shrugged as though it was funny. "I've just been worried about Yankees all day long."

The marchand nodded, resting his oars across his knees. "Word has it they are on their way to Texas quick as they can, but our boys are forming up to engage again. Or so folks are saying who have been down closer to Vermilionville."

Amelina nodded, trying not to glance at the thinnest layer of moss that covered the Yankee's face. If the marchand came any nearer, he would be close enough to notice the odd shape of her load.

"I've talked to a number of men since I left your place and they all say the same thing," the marchand told her, his eyes intent. "The Yankees have destroyed most of what they have passed through. You all had best hope they don't decide to come this way."

"That's what you said this morning," Amelina said, fighting an insistent urge to paddle away from this man as fast as she could. His low, confiding voice grated on her nerves.

The marchand maneuvered his bateau to come up even with her. "If they do come up the bayou, the smartest thing you can do is get out. Do you have someone you could go stay with?"

Amelina nodded stiffly, afraid to look at him. "I do. Thank you for your concern, sir." She forced herself to smile in his direction. "But I ought to be going on home and—"

"I tell you what," the marchand interrupted her. "I have to go back up by your place anyway, so I will just see you home. I'm in no hurry," he added, when he saw her shaking her head.

"There's really no need for you to do that," Amelina began, but he raised one hand to stop her.

"I have a daughter about your age. And that uncle of yours should keep a closer eye on you, young lady. It isn't proper to have you going back and forth like this on your own."

Amelina shook her head, frantically trying to think of something to say. "But, really, I don't wish to trouble you and—"

"It's no bother at all," the marchand said. He worked one oar, turning his bateau so that they were parallel in the water. Amelina forced herself not to glance down at the moss, terrified her nervousness would show and he would begin to wonder why.

Then he made the sort of gesture a man would make at a fais do-do, to avoid bumping into someone.

With a mock bow, he indicated he would wait politely while she went first.

Trying to hide the uneasiness that was tightening her stomach and making her hands sweat, Amelina put her paddle in the water and started off. The marchand rowed along just behind her. She tried to keep a steady pace that wouldn't seem odd to him. But with every measured stroke of her oar, she bit her lip. What if the Yankee had fallen unconscious under the moss? What would happen if he woke up and forgot where he was and why?

As if in answer to her thoughts, Amelina felt two quick taps on her ankle and glanced down to see his boot toe disappearing back beneath the piles of silvery green moss. She glanced back. The marchand was too close for her to speak anything aloud without him hearing her voice, if not her words.

She rowed three hard strokes, trying to put a little distance between her pirogue and the bateau behind her. She could see the Yankee's closed right eye—but only because she knew exactly where to look. Was he conscious? Or had he just moved a little in his pain?

"Hey!" the marchand called out. "I never introduced myself, did I?"

Amelina shook her head.

"My name is Sawyer. Isaac Sawyer."

"I'm Amelina Carrett," Amelina responded,

trying to force her voice into casualness. "Nice to meet you."

"Nice to meet you, too," the marchand answered.

"I appreciate your time," Amelina said, forcing a smile as she turned to look at him.

He nodded. "Like I said, I'm in no hurry. When we get to your place, I'll help you get that moss inside."

Amelina felt her heart sink. She kept smiling, trying to think of something to say. Finally, she shook her head and let the pirogue drop back a little so she didn't have to shout. "Oh, no," Amelina said. "There's no need at all for you to do that."

"Like I said, I am in no hurry. And you'll want to get it in quick." He pointed straight upward.

Amelina followed his gesture. For the first time she noticed that the sun had disappeared behind an advancing layer of gray clouds. Along the southern horizon, the clouds were even darker and thicker.

"Looks like we might get some rain," Mr. Sawyer said.

Amelina nodded numbly and began to paddle again.

CHAPTER EIGHT

Amelina led Mr. Sawyer slowly down the bayou. With his double oars and his flat-bottomed bateau, he could have gone much faster than she could even if she had been trying. She kept waiting for him to get impatient, to ask if she could speed up some, but he didn't.

"Those are some fine old magnolias," he said loudly enough for her to hear as they came up onto the La Fleur place.

"They certainly are," Amelina called back to him, trying to sound lighthearted. She said a little prayer, asking the saints and the mother of Jesus to please make this kindly man go away and leave her alone.

Amelina looked down at the moss. It was harder to see the Yankee's face through the thinnest part now that the sun had dimmed. But that wasn't going to be of much help—not if Mr. Sawyer insisted on helping her carry the moss in. If he did that, nothing would help.

"You just cook up a meal for yourself every evening?" Mr. Sawyer was saying.

Amelina started to nod before she thought about his reasons for asking. Then she quickly shook her head. "Not most nights, no," she said over her shoulder. "I just eat cold salt pork or some cold beans." She shook her head. "Saves a lot of firewood, eating cold like that."

The bayou was widening and Mr. Sawyer pulled harder on his oars. When Amelina realized what he was doing, she put her back into paddling, but it was useless. The bateau caught up and kept beside her easily. She glanced at the layers of moss, then looked away quickly. They didn't have much farther to go now. She had to think of some way to make Mr. Sawyer leave her at the dock.

"You say you have relatives close by?" he asked abruptly.

Amelina nodded slightly, wondering why he thought it was his affair to know where her family lived.

"A brother or sister? Or more cousins?" he persisted.

Amelina turned around. "I thank you again for your help and concern, Mr. Sawyer, but I will be fine at my own house. I always am."

"I was just thinking with this storm coming and all—"

"I am not afraid of storms," Amelina said quickly, shaking her head, but he went on anyway.

"I thought if you cared to stay with family tonight, I might ask if I could take shelter at your uncle's farm. Just for tonight," he added quickly, then pulled two or three oar strokes to catch up, looking at her.

Amelina stared at him. His face was perfectly sincere, his eyes direct and straightforward. She was positive he meant no more by what he was asking than exactly what he had said. Tante Rosemarie had sent him across the river, after all. She got strong feelings about people and if she had sensed anything dangerous or even dishonest about this man, she would never have done that. Amelina wished she could confide in the marchand, ask him for help taking care of the Yankee. But that was impossible, of course.

"I'm sorry, Mr. Sawyer," she said clearly and firmly. "I have to be at home tonight. I have a sow I have to keep watch on." She turned to face him. "Maybe Tante Honorine and her husband would let you stay."

"I'd sleep in a barn," Mr. Sawyer said. "All I want is somewhere out of the wet. Someplace to keep my goods dry until the storm goes through."

"Maybe Tante Honorine can help you," Amelina repeated.

Mr. Sawyer nodded, then pointed as they rounded the last bend. "That's your place, isn't it?"

Amelina returned his nod, glancing down at the

sliver of black boot that showed between the lacelike strands of Spanish moss. "I might just leave the moss in the pirogue until I've done some chores," she said, a little too loudly, as she switched the paddle back and forth, taking two strokes on the outside, the face of the paddle slanted to angle the direction of the pirogue more sharply. Off to the south, there was a distant rumble of thunder. It was barely audible, but a tiny sparkle of lightning told Amelina she hadn't imagined it.

"I don't think it's going to be long before it rains," Mr. Sawyer cautioned.

Amelina shrugged, wishing he would just take his leave of her and go.

"Is that Tante Honorine's place?" He lifted one oar to point across the river.

"No," Amelina told him quickly. "That one is my tante Rosemarie. Tante Honorine lives a ways up the bayou—it's a big farm with a long galerie and a row of lilac bushes out front." Amelina kept her eyes straight ahead. Tante Rosemarie probably would offer him a place to wait out the storm, but she didn't want him to be nearby.

"I recall seeing the lilacs," Mr. Sawyer said, then looked up at the sky again. He fell back a little as Amelina rowed a straight line for the end of the dock. She glanced back at him, hoping he would just wave and go on, but he followed her in.

"Thank you for seeing me home safe," Amelina said, sitting still in her pirogue.

Mr. Sawyer was maneuvering his bateau alongside the dock, the side of his boat bumping against the end pylon. As Amelina watched, helpless to do anything else, he got out of his bateau and tied it to one of the iron hooks pegged into the planks. As he stood looking at her expectantly, rain began to fall.

"Just up on the galerie is all right?" Mr. Sawyer asked, gesturing at the moss. He extended his hand to help her out of the pirogue. He was so close—too close. What would he do if he saw the Yankee? She glanced at his bateau. There, in the stern, next to a rolled jacket, lying on top of what looked like a bedroll, was a smoothbore rifle, the angular, heavy stock clean and polished.

Amelina stood up and tried desperately to think of something to say, but she couldn't. There was just no logical reason to leave good fresh moss out in the weather. It would stand a much bigger chance of molding if it got wet at all. Any fool knew that and she could hardly pretend not to. The rain increased a little.

"Come on, Amelina," Mr. Sawyer said. He sounded impatient now that the rain had begun.

Amelina nodded vaguely, saying another prayer as she swayed to her feet, knowing the instant she was out of the way Mr. Sawyer would bend down to gather up an armload of moss. She felt three quick taps on her ankle and caught her breath. If the Yankee was going to start moving now, there would be no chance of hiding him. Or was he trying to tell her something?

"Here," Amelina said suddenly, bending to scoop up an armload of the moss from where it lay thickest across the Yankee's legs. Careful not to take too much, she swung around, the pirogue rocking, extending the load to Mr. Sawyer. He bent to take it from her, then turned and strode toward the house. She watched him jump lightly off the end of the dock, clearing the mud puddle. Then he went up the rise and disappeared on the far side of the levee.

"Are you awake?" Amelina hissed.

"I am," the Yankee answered. "Where has he gone?"

"To the house," Amelina answered. "He will be back in a minute or perhaps two."

"He is a loyal Confederate?" the Yankee asked.

"Yes." Amelina glanced toward the house. "Can you get out of the pirogue alone?"

There was a second's hesitation, then the Yankee answered. "Maybe. I'd better."

"Hide under the dock," Amelina told him.

She didn't give the Yankee time to answer. Bending to rake together an armload of moss, she almost fell turning around. Then she hurried toward the house. Halfway up the path, she saw Mr. Sawyer coming back.

"Here!" she sang out merrily, extending both arms, offering him the moss.

For a terrible instant, Amelina thought he wasn't going to take it.

Then, shrugging his shirt higher as the force of the rain increased once more, he did. The moment he had turned around, Amelina sprinted back up the slope of the levee, then back down to the dock.

The Yankee had managed to sit up, but he was breathing hard, his face pale and flecked with soft moss. Amelina bent to help him, but he shook his head fiercely.

"Just keep him up at the house," he whispered, and Amelina saw the moss shift as he bent his knees, grunting with pain and effort. "Can you—keep him away?"

"Yes. I think so." Amelina knelt to drag an armful of moss toward herself. Then she stood quickly and ran again, leaping over the puddle, digging her feet into the soft dirt to sprint up the side of the levee.

"You have a lot of spunk for the end of a hard day." Mr. Sawyer laughed when he saw her running toward him.

Amelina smiled, looking past him up the path. There was a mound of moss on the planked floor of the galerie. The rain was noisy on the roof now and she could smell the sharp odor of the wet bousillage of the walls and chimney.

"We could wait out the shower," she said, hoping he would agree and make things easier. But he shook his head, rubbing his forehead with one hand.

"You can if you like," he said kindly. "I think I will just go on and finish up. What's left? Six or eight armloads?"

"Maybe about that," Amelina said, thrusting the moss she was carrying into his chest so he had to take it or let it fall. He looked startled, but before he had time to speak, she turned and headed back down the path.

The Yankee was on his hands and knees on the dock when Amelina came over the top of the levee. She glanced behind herself at the retreating back of the marchand, then sprinted downward, toward the pirogue.

"Let me help you up," she said to the Yankee. This time, he nodded and waited until she was crouched, holding his right arm before he tried to stand. As he rose, Amelina stood with him, taking as much of his weight as she could. The rain was cold dripping down the back of her neck where it had soaked through her bonnet.

The Yankee managed to stay upright, but he stood swaying, his eyes squeezed shut for an instant. Then he opened them and began to walk. He took longer steps this time and Amelina could hear the effort it cost him in the sharp intake of his breath.

"How long have I . . . got?" the Yankee asked, and Amelina could only shake her head.

"Not long. Another minute. No more than that. He's in a hurry to get it unloaded."

The Yankee looked down at the drop-off at the end of the dock and the shallow puddle just past it. "You better . . . go," he said unevenly.

Amelina was afraid to move away from him, sure he couldn't walk on his own, but she knew he was right. Mr. Sawyer would be coming back any second.

Amelina stiffened when the Yankee lifted his arm from her shoulders and took a step. He staggered to one side and she started to catch his arm again, but he shook his head at her, grimacing. He gestured. "Go on." Frantic, Amelina spun away from him and pounded back out to the end of the dock. She fell to her knees and leaned out over the pirogue to scoop moss into her arms.

Clutching it to her chest, Amelina ran the length of the dock once more. The Yankee had moved to one side and stood unsteadily as she passed him. He looked faint, whiter than hulled rice, but he motioned her on and she was afraid to stop, even for another instant.

Amelina jumped from the planks to the ground, landing lightly on the far side of the wide mud puddle. Without looking back she sprinted up the side of the levee and very nearly ran into the marchand.

"Whoa!" he said good-naturedly as she stumbled to a halt. "I was right to keep going, wasn't I?"

She looked at him blankly and he pointed skyward. "It has let up."

Amelina nodded. It had. He was right. She held out the moss. He tilted his head and gave her a puzzled glance, then took it and turned back toward the house. Only then did Amelina dare to look back out toward the dock.

She was far enough down the slope of the levee that she couldn't see over it. Mr. Sawyer was a lot taller than she was, but if he had spotted the Yankee, she was sure he would have reacted. Amelina let out a long breath. Starting toward her pirogue, she glanced back at Mr. Sawyer and saw him stepping onto the house path. He would only be another moment or two, then he would start this way again. Amelina broke back into a run.

"Amelina?" Mr. Sawyer shouted from the house.

She slid to a halt one step away from the top of the levee and turned again to face him. He was standing beneath the galerie roof, back by the loft stairs, his hands on his hips.

"Did you go hunting today?"

She started to shake her head, but an inner voice told her not to and she stopped herself.

"Did you get a rabbit or something?"

Amelina nodded, a slight, tentative motion that

she wasn't sure he could even see, standing as far away as he was. She was pretty sure she knew why he was asking. If she said she had killed a rabbit, how was she going to explain where the carcass had gone? Would he ask? Or maybe he would assume she had made a fire and roasted it. Or would he notice her untouched meal basket in the stern?

When she didn't answer, he held out the moss she had given him. "There's blood on it. Do you want me to hang that part over the rail and let the next downpour wash it?"

Amelina nodded, a big exaggerated gesture he couldn't miss. "Thank you," she called, then turned and walked up the levee, her knees feeling like India rubber, as if her legs might give way at any moment.

At the top she could see that the dock was empty, but still she waited, taking three more steps down the slope to make sure that Mr. Sawyer couldn't possibly see her. Then she ran again.

CHAPTER NINE

"Where are you?" Amelina called softly as she got closer. Instead of jumping back up onto the planked dock, she walked around it, bending to look beneath the boards where the land slanted down to the water. "Are you all right?" she whispered.

There was no response.

Amelina stared into the shadows, making out the curve of a black boot. But it was toe down, as though the Yankee had fallen face first into the mud. She took one step forward, her hand over her mouth.

"Did you lose something?"

Amelina straightened and turned to see Mr. Sawyer. He was standing on top of the levee now, his hands on his hips. She was furious with herself for being so foolish. She walked toward the marchand. "I'm sorry. I am not keeping up with you, am I?"

Mr. Sawyer laughed. "Moss is not very heavy, Miss Amelina."

The rain suddenly spattered down a little harder

and Amelina shrugged her shoulders against the cool drops as she climbed the slope and stood at the end of the dock, looking at Mr. Sawyer. "I can finish up," she said hopefully.

He shook his head. "There can't be too much more, can there? Let's just get it done and then you can go get dry."

Amelina started to argue with him, then didn't, knowing it was probably useless. And if she argued too much against a polite offer of help, he might begin to wonder what she was up to. Forcing a smile, she clambered onto the end of the dock, suddenly aware of her muddy feet and spattered dress. Mr. Sawyer stepped up right behind her.

Amelina led the way, the wet planks slippery now that the rain had gotten heavy again. She glanced upward to see that the clouds had thickened, their gray bellies hanging low.

The pirogue was still snug against the dock and Amelina let out a relieved breath when she saw that there really wasn't very much more moss inside it. That same breath came back in sharply as she saw the dark circle of blood on the silver green in the bow of the boat. She turned, glancing back over her shoulder, and positioned herself between the stain and Mr. Sawyer.

Bending forward to scoop the soiled moss into a pile, she quickly flipped it over, then maneuvered it onto a thick mat of the spongy soft stuff. Gathering the whole mass into her arms, she struggled to her feet.

Mr. Sawyer was gazing down the bayou. The water was peppered with tiny, overlapping rings spreading out from each raindrop. "Can you manage that much?" he asked, turning to face her.

"Yes." Amelina glanced down into the bottom of the pirogue, holding her breath. She had missed a little blood—not much. If Mr. Sawyer saw it, he didn't say anything as he bent to pull free some of the moss she had packed into the sides of the bow.

Hoping to get at least a little ahead of him, Amelina started down the dock, walking as fast as she could. Her jump across the puddle at the end was graceless and she staggered a little, but didn't fall. Nearly running, she hurried up the levee, then back down onto the house path.

When she reached the galerie, Amelina dumped the moss onto the floor, on the far side of the loft stairs, glancing around wildly, trying to think where she could hide it. Then she glanced back toward the levee and stood still. It was too late. Mr. Sawyer was already on his way.

Amelina forced herself to walk away from the pile of moss and nodded at Mr. Sawyer as she passed him on the path. The rain was really pelting down now and she ran with her shoulders hunched up, wondering if the Yankee had managed to sit beneath the dock or if he was still sprawled in the mud.

Knowing there was no solution other than getting Mr. Sawyer to leave as quickly as possible, Amelina snatched up another load of moss and ran for the galerie. Mr. Sawyer passed her, his head low, his jacket collar turned up to keep the rain off his neck.

Amelina dumped her load of moss on the planks, relieved to see he had piled his next to her previous load without disturbing it. Then she turned to race back out into the rain.

When she didn't see him coming toward her halfway to the levee, Amelina wondered if Mr. Sawyer had just gotten into his bateau and was waiting to bid her farewell. She felt her heart rising with hope as she hurried, taking long strides up the slope. Then, at the top of the levee, her heart constricted.

Mr. Sawyer had not gotten back into his bateau—nor was he standing on the dock. He was on the bank of the bayou to the side of it. He wasn't looking beneath it, he was gazing out over the water again. But if he turned, if the Yankee moved, or made a sound . . .

"Come down here a second, will you?" Mr. Sawyer called.

Amelina hurried forward, skirting the dock to run the few paces down the slope beside it, standing between Mr. Sawyer and the cypress pilings that supported the dock. If the Yankee was beneath the dock now—and he had to be—Mr. Sawyer was standing no more than five paces away from him.

"Do you hear that?"

Amelina could hear little above the pounding of her heart, but she listened for a few seconds, praying the Yankee would make no sound at all until she could get this nosy, well-intentioned man to leave.

"There," the marchand said. "Do you hear that?"

Amelina shook her head, honestly puzzled, her heart still thudding. The Yankee had made no sound, she was sure.

"That's gunfire again," Mr. Sawyer said. He shook his head and rain flew from his hat brim. "Damn Yankees. I hope our boys stop 'em where they stand." There was such hatred in his voice that it scared Amelina as much as the idea that the gunfire had started up again.

"I can't hear anything," she said quietly.

Mr. Sawyer turned to face her. The rain was dripping down his cheeks like tears. "Well, I suppose you will be safe enough tonight. It's a long way off and there is a lot of swamp and a lot of 'gators between here and there—and the Yankees won't likely travel in the wet." He wiped at the rain on his face. "Your uncle will be back tomorrow?"

Amelina nodded. "I hope so." She shivered, chilled and uneasy. She had never told so many half lies in her whole life. She had no idea when Nonc Alain was returning. She would say prayers tonight and confess the next time she got to go to church.

"I hate leaving you here by yourself," Mr. Sawyer said.

Amelina didn't answer, but she smiled at him, willing him to leave. He was a nice man and a kind man, and she just wanted him to get in his bateau and disappear up the bayou.

"How far is this aunt of yours?"

"Upstream, around the big bend, then past the shallows a ways," Amelina said a little too loudly.

"The place with the lilacs," he said, waiting for her to nod. Finally he touched his hat. "You take good care, now, miss," he said.

"I thank you for your concern," she said again.

He touched his hat brim once more and turned to walk slowly past her, back up onto the dock. Amelina forced herself to stand very still until he had finally untied his bateau, and rowing hard with one oar, turned it around. He waved and Amelina waved back at him. Then she turned around and walked toward the house. Once she was over the hump of the levee, where Mr. Sawyer could not glance back and see her, she began to run.

Pushing open the door, Amelina crossed to the hearth, pulling off her sodden bonnet. She hung it on the drying pegs, then used the iron poker to stir the ashes and smiled when two or three oyster-sized coals emerged. She pushed them together, their sides touching, and leaned to blow on them.

Seeing her breath answered by a bright red glow, she rocked back on her heels and scooped a double handful of dried corncobs from the kindling box and laid them crisscross on top. Then she leaned down to blow again. A twisting spire of thick white smoke began to rise, disappearing up the chimney. Amelina blew harder, until flames crackled into being. Then she added some small pine splits.

Standing up, Amelina crossed the room in four long strides and undid the latch on the back door. The rain was still coming down hard. She ran to the wood-pile and loaded her arms full, whirling back to carry it inside. She made two trips, then added bigger wood to her load. After five trips, she had a good pile of firewood beside the hearth. She fed the growing flames, then ran toward the front door. Mr. Sawyer had to be out of sight by now.

Close to topping the levee, Amelina slowed down, breathing hard. A fresh spate of rain fell, making her realize she had forgotten to put her bonnet back on—not that it would have been any drier. She glanced across the bayou. Tante Rosemarie had not come back out. Glancing upstream she saw that Mr. Sawyer was almost out of sight.

Amelina held still a few seconds longer as the

curve in the bayou finally made the bateau disappear from sight. The instant it did, she sprinted toward the dock, then veered to follow her own deep, muddy footprints alongside it.

"Are you all right?" she whispered, somehow still afraid to call out to the Yankee.

There was no answer—or at least none she could hear over the shushing sound of the falling rain. She waded into the cold mud, lifting her hem. She looked down at herself and winced. Her poor dress was filthy, the hem full of grass seed and mud.

"Are you here?" Amelina called again, bending low to look beneath the dock. The afternoon shadows were lengthening now and it was hard to see.

Amelina stooped, ducking between the cypress pilings, hoping to see the Yankee sitting up, looking at her steadily—but dreading the opposite, that he would be lying facedown still, perhaps even dead from the exertion. It took her a long moment to realize that neither her hope nor her fear would come to pass. The Yankee was not there at all.

CHAPTER TEN

Amelina stood still for a second, unsure what to do. Then she spun around and ran out between the pylons to the water's edge, scanning the rain-pocked surface of the bayou. If he had fallen in, he would have drowned, she was sure. A man who could barely walk would not be able to swim for more than a few seconds.

"I should never have left him," Amelina said aloud, anguished that after everything the Yankee had been through, he had died in the end from her foolishness. "I should have refused Mr. Sawyer's help or just turned around and headed downstream again or something . . ."

Her eyes were burning as she scanned the water's surface, her tears diluted by the rainwater that ran down her face. She followed the water's edge, walking downstream past the garden. Staying below the levee so that it was unlikely anyone would see her from a front galerie, she walked almost a mile. Finally, she gave up. She was fighting a sense of terrible sadness as she walked back alongside the dock and made her way up out of the mud onto the grassy slope of the levee.

Shivering, going slowly, Amelina got her meal basket out of the stern, only then remembering the Yankee's canteen and hat were hidden inside it. Climbing the levee, she dragged her feet through the wet grass to get rid of some of the clinging mud. She dreaded seeing the hat and the canteen. What would she do with them? Bury them? The idea made her sadness sharp and painful.

As Amelina got closer to the galerie, she saw she had left the front door standing wide open—even though she thought she could recall closing it behind herself. That meant whatever warmth her little fire had created had all been lost.

Even though this was a small thing compared to all else that had happened, Amelina suddenly began to cry again. It seemed as though everything was mixed up and wrong. After all her lying and trying, the Yankee had still lost his life.

The rain suddenly increased into a pounding downpour and Amelina ran the last few steps, ducking under the galerie roof. She used the streams of water pouring from the eaves to wash her hands and arms, then stood on one foot at a time to rinse the last of the mud from her legs.

When she finally turned, shivering violently, and picked up her basket again, her tears had stopped. She still felt terribly sad, but somehow the sharpness of it had subsided, leaving an ache she was more able to stand.

Amelina closed the door behind herself, then glanced at the hearth, sure her little fire had gone out by now. She caught her breath in astonishment when she saw the flames leaping around several small logs piled onto the fire. Then she noticed a trail of spattered water and mud across the floor.

An instant later Amelina saw the Yankee in the shadows just outside the firelight. He was sitting up, more or less, his back propped against the side wall of the house. His head was down, his chin resting on his chest.

Amelina ran toward him, leaving wet footprints on the planks. She knelt down, looking into his face. Even as she stared at him, she could feel the warmth of the fire through her wet clothing.

"Are you all right?"

He opened his eyes and lifted his head. "Better here than in the rain. Much better."

"I thought you . . . I thought—"

"I was hiding in your corn patch," he interrupted her. "I saw you headed downstream. I tried to shout." He stopped a moment and pulled in two long breaths. "I couldn't." A quivering in his voice made

Amelina realize he was shivering even harder than she was.

"My uncle has dry clothes you can put on," Amelina said, and the Yankee's eyes lit up. "And I have cloth for a bandage and salt pork stew and—"

"And you are an angel," the Yankee said, then grimaced.

Amelina stood still for a second, her hands clenched, then ran across the room to the door that led into Nonc Alain's boudoir. On the highest shelf of his armoire were his winter trousers of heavy brown wool. He had left three of his shirts. Amelina took the oldest and most worn. Then she opened his small drawer of socks and chose a warm, heavy-knit pair of *chausson* Tante Honorine had given Nonc Alain as a gift.

Carrying the little stack of clean clothes out in front of herself to keep them from touching her own soaked and muddy dress, Amelina went back into the front room. "Can you—" she began, holding out the clothes.

"Get my boots," the Yankee said slowly, "I can do the rest."

Shivering, Amelina knelt as he stretched out his legs.

"No," he said. Amelina looked into his face. "You're freezing. Get yourself dry first."

Amelina shook her head and lifted his foot, hooking two fingers beneath the muddy heel. She rocked backward, pulling hard, and the boot slid off. She set it by the fire and the leather began to steam almost instantly. Amelina took off the Yankee's other boot, then straightened.

Her shivering had escalated and she was shuddering now, her legs trembling, her teeth chattering. It was cold, yes, but she knew it was something more, too. She was afraid. Not of the Yankee—she could see decency and kindness in his face and eyes. He had seemed as worried about her welfare as he was his own. But just having him here . . . what if the hounds led the Confederates to her door?

The Yankee made a sound of pain, low in his throat, as he leaned forward to pull the clothes closer. Amelina saw the dark stain on the front of his jacket and inhaled sharply. "I forgot a bandage. I have some clean cotton rags I can cut and—"

"Go get dry," he interrupted her.

Amelina shook her head, then nodded. Her thoughts felt as trembly and shaky as the rest of her. The soldier smiled a little and gestured her away, then reached for Nonc Alain's trousers.

Amelina turned and walked to her own boudoir door, went in, and closed it behind herself. For a moment she could only stand there, her teeth still chattering. Then she crossed her arms and reached down to pull her dress over her head.

Just getting the wet material off her skin helped.

She dried herself with the thick soft cloth she used after her Saturday baths, blotting her hair and rubbing at her skin until she turned pink. By the time she had pulled off her soaked chemise and her underdrawers, she had stopped shivering.

Amelina opened her own armoire. Her remaining two dresses hung on the side that opened correctly. The other side stopped halfway. The hinge was broken.

The brightly striped dress was for church only. Tante Honorine had woven the cloth and Tante Rosemarie had done the sewing. Amelina had made the other one, with help. It was as plain as the one she had gotten muddy. The natural brownish white of the cotton was unchanged from the day she had picked the bolls from the cotton patch behind the house. She had woven the cloth and Tante Honorine had helped her cut it. She and Perrine had done all the sewing.

Amelina pulled the dress off its hook. It was not a fancy cut. She had let down the hem so it was still long enough. But the sleeves were too short, riding well above her wrist bones. As she pulled her clean chemise over her head, she wished she had made herself another dress before this. The Yankee would be sure she was a poor, neglected child.

She wondered where he was from, what his name was, if he was used to fine things and fancy clothes like the sugar plantation families on Bayou

Lafourche or farther south on Bayou Teche, or the wealthy ship owners down in New Orleans.

Hopping in a circle as she almost lost her balance pulling on her dry drawers, Amelina scolded herself. There was no need to hurry now. Once she had tied the drawstrings on her underwear and had slipped her dress over her head, she just stood by the door, listening, afraid to open it. How long would it take him to get dressed? Could he manage without help? She pressed her ear against the pinewood of the door planks, but she couldn't hear anything.

Turning her ragbag upside down over her bed, Amelina found half an old bedcover. She had used the other half to make a cotton sack the fall before. Working quickly, she tore the soft, worn cloth into strips a handspan wide. Then she rolled them into a loose ball, starting a new piece every time an old one was used up, overlapping the ends so they wouldn't unravel.

Then she went back and stood by the door again. Shifting her cold bare feet restlessly on the floor, Amelina finally pushed the door open an inch and spoke through the crack. "May I come out?"

"Yes."

The Yankee's voice was soft, but distinct. Amelina pushed her door open and saw him sitting before the fire, shirtless and wearing Nonc Alain's trousers, his own clothes a muddy heap beside him.

His boots were on the hearth, still steaming as the leather heated up. "I hated to ruin the shirt," he said unevenly, looking down at the thin trickle of blood that oozed from his wound.

Amelina crossed the room, the ball of bandage cloth in her hand. It wasn't the small, evil-looking hole a rifle ball made. It was a gash as long as her index finger in the center of his chest. He looked up and saw her staring. "Bayonet," he told her. "I turned just in time."

Amelina nodded to show him she understood, afraid to trust her own voice. She had seen hunting accidents, men hurt working, children too young to play with knives cut when they tried to imitate older brothers and sisters playing mumblety-peg—but this was the first time she had ever seen anyone who had been hurt by someone *trying* to kill him. Somehow it made the gash worse, more frightening.

"Bleeding's about done, I think," the soldier was saying. "Mostly anyhow."

Amelina nodded and met his eyes. His color was coming back a little. Maybe he had been exhausted and cold and scared as much as he had been hurt. He pointed at the ball of cotton strips.

"Bandages?"

She nodded.

He put out his hand. "Here."

Amelina handed him the ball and went to carry

his clothes out to soak in the washtub in the cuisine. When she came back, she watched as he slowly unwound the first three strips and folded them up into a thick padding that he placed over the wound, leaning back so it wouldn't fall.

Then he held out the bandages to her again. "Do the first one?"

He said no more, but it was obvious what he meant. There was no way he could wrap the bandage around himself and hold the pad over his wound at the same time.

Amelina sat on the floor beside him, tugging her hemline down to cover her ankles. She took a deep breath. If she wanted to be a traiteur, even to be among the girls Tante Rosemarie would consider as her successor, she had to build a stronger nerve.

She tied two of the bandage strips together and wound the cloth around the Yankee's torso, passing it over the wadded cotton strips he had placed on the wound. She went around him twice, then secured the ends with a tight knot as she had seen Tante Rosemarie do many times.

When the Yankee tried to take the ball of cotton strips from her hands, it was obvious how much it hurt him to move. So Amelina finished the job, going as quickly as she could, blushing furiously the whole time. The Yankee was kind enough to sit still and remain silent until she was finished. Then he slowly and awkwardly slid Nonc Alain's shirt over his head and pulled it straight.

Then he seemed to collapse in on himself. He swayed and fell to one side. Amelina tried to catch him, but he was too heavy for her. She could only break his fall so that he didn't hit his head.

"I'm sorry, miss," he said quietly. Then he fell silent.

Amelina slid her hands from beneath his shoulder and rocked back on her heels, thinking. He needed to stay by the fire, but lying on the cold hard planks would be miserable for a man already in so much pain.

Running to Nonc Alain's boudoir again, she pulled the top mattress from his bed and dragged it through the doorway, the moss rustling inside. When the Yankee saw her, he shook his head, but when she positioned the mattress beside him, he rolled onto it, sighing in relief.

Amelina built up the hearth fire a little more, then stood back. "Are you hungry?" Amelina asked the Yankee.

His eyes flew open. "Yes. I haven't eaten in . . . "

He trailed off and Amelina could see he was trying to recall his last meal. "Two days," he said finally. Then he closed his eyes again.

"I'll get you some stew heated up," Amelina told him. He opened his eyes wearily and smiled. "What's your name, angel of mercy?"

She blushed again, almost sure Father Le Blanc would think it was sacrilege to let him tease her about angels like this. "Amelina Carrett."

"Michael Reed is grateful to you, Amelina. You have saved his life."

With that, Mr. Reed closed his eyes again and Amelina jumped up, grabbing the meal basket she had left sitting inside the door. She set the Yankee's hat on the hearth to dry, his canteen beside it. Then, she went out. Once she was outside, she ran the few steps across the galerie—the wind had picked up and was swirling spatters of rain beneath the roofline. Pushing the basket handle over her forearm, she opened the latch on the cuisine door. She put the salt pork away, but she kept the corn bread out.

The stew pot was heavy, but she picked it up along with a ladle and two tin plates. Tending two fires would be too hard, and there was a pothook in the house hearth as well. In weather like this—when a fire would not drive them from the room on an already hot night—she often cooked indoors.

Staggering a little under the weight of the iron pot and everything she had stacked on top of it, Amelina went back inside. Mr. Reed opened his eyes to watch her hang the pot, half sitting up when she faltered a little.

"I can do it," she told him.

He sank back down with a little exhalation. She

gave him a piece of the corn bread and he ate it eagerly, still lying down. When the pot began to bubble, he turned slowly onto his side to face the hearth, and Amelina could see a wolfish appetite gleam in his eyes. When she ladled out the bubbling stew, he sat up again, reaching for the plate before he was steady.

As hot as the stew was, he finished his bowl and half the corn bread before she had eaten her portion. Amelina saw him glance at the pot.

"There's plenty," she told him.

The second bowl went down slower, and Amelina found herself watching him eat even though she knew it was rude.

"What?" he asked, looking up and meeting her eyes.

"I can't help but wonder why you ended up out there all alone like that."

He nodded. "Guess you would," he said, and his voice was steadier, stronger.

He said no more. Amelina waited until he had finished the stew and set his bowl aside. When he still didn't speak, she got up and went out to the cuisine to fill the dish tin. Coming back in, she switched it for the stew pot and set the water to heating so she could wash up. Mr. Reed lay back down and was still and silent for so long that Amelina finally understood he was asleep. The room seemed unnaturally silent. The rain was letting up, too.

Amelina gathered the dirty dishes and carried them out to the washbasin in the cuisine, then went back for the tin tub of hot water. But the whole time she was doing chores, she was thinking furiously about what she was going to do next.

She couldn't just leave Mr. Reed lying in front of the hearth for as long as it took him to recover. Anyone who came onto the galerie in the day could open the door and see him there. But where could she let him sleep? The logical place was the loft, but he couldn't possibly manage the steep outside stairs.

Amelina made quick work of the dishes and set the rack over the basin, stacking them on it to dry. Then she went to let the hen with chicks out of the coop for a few hours before sunset. Vagabond was clucking and grousing in the palmetto along the side of the low pasture, and Amelina chased him and his hens back into the yard. At least he had not gone too far today, and Amelina was grateful for that. They could not afford to lose their chickens. Especially now when Nonc Alain seemed to have given up farming.

Amelina found six eggs beneath the old wagon with the broken axle that sat behind the house and noticed it was time to cut more grass and put it underneath. The hens liked it thick so they could nestle in it, hollowing out bowl-shaped nests. Amelina checked the other places, too: the dirt and weed-choked V of the old plowshare that sat rusting behind the unused mule shed; the pile of palmetto Nonc Alain had cut, intending to make hats to sell; then finally, she looked beneath the edge of the galerie planks.

With eighteen eggs swinging in her skirt, she went back into the cuisine and set them carefully in the wire baskets that hung from the ceiling, glad there would be plenty for Mr. Reed to eat. Amelina had heard Tante Rosemarie tell her patients that eggs would make them strong.

A quick check of the pigs relieved Amelina of a nagging worry. The purebred sow had not gone into labor. She was up and rooting around her trough.

As Amelina went back into the house, Mr. Reed opened his eyes. "There are lots of eggs for supper later on," she told him. "And the rain has let up."

"Are you still wondering?" he asked her.

She nodded and he motioned for her to come closer. She sat on an overturned bucket and he began to talk without sitting up.

"I got into the army almost two years ago. In Ohio."

Amelina waited politely when he paused and took a deep breath before he went on.

"We were on our way to . . . " he trailed off, and Amelina leaned forward.

"Texas," she said. "Everyone knows that."

Mr. Reed laughed, a pained, hoarse laugh that made him clutch at himself. He shook his head. "We thought it was a military secret," he managed. Then he fell silent again and Amelina waited.

"I was supposed to be traipsing around with my spyglass, to see where the Louisiana volunteers camped. I do hate slavery," he added, his voice suddenly strained and angry. "It is the wrongest thing on this earth, to my mind."

Amelina thought of all the slaves she had seen on her two trips to Vermilionville, working in the fields, their faces blank with heat and weariness. She shivered, even though she was no longer cold.

"It's bad for them and bad for their owners," Mr. Reed went on. "It's bad for children to see grown folks scolded like babies or whipped like animals. There's not a single good aspect."

Amelina could see the fervor in his eyes and knew he was an abolitionist. She had heard of them, but she had never met one. She knew a lot of people who didn't like slavery, who thought it was wrong, but no one here ever thought it could just be ended. Mr. Reed did.

"We have never had a slave on the place," she said, defending herself against the hatred she saw in his face. "Tante Rosemarie says God hates slave owners and Nonc Alain says it's wrong, too."

"They should help the Union, then," Mr. Reed said carefully. Amelina looked at him. He looked like a simple man, but he wasn't. He was an abolitionist and a spy—both things were as strange and foreign to her as mountains.

"Have you ever seen a mountain?" she asked him impulsively, watching his face intently, hoping he would let her steer him away from talking about helping the Yankees win the war.

He laughed. "I have. We followed along the foothills of the Smokies and the Blues coming down here. Crossed another range they didn't tell us the name of."

"Are they big?" Amelina asked him.

He nodded. "Bigger than you can imagine. They fill the sky."

Amelina could not keep from staring at him, thinking about anything being big enough to fill the sky. He was silent, gazing into the flames. "What does a spy do?" she asked finally, just to keep him talking.

"Well, I had drawings and maps and notes made up about creeks and bridges and how many Confederates were in which places. I was about to slip back to the Union boys' camp . . . " He took a deep breath and started talking again. "But I got so tired and so hungry I fell asleep a-spying."

Mr. Reed stopped again to breathe, his fingers rubbing the left side of his shirt where the wad of cotton rags protected his wound now. "They got me," he said. "I woke up staring down that bayonet and I rolled just in time to make it angle off my breastbone."

He winced as he sat up. "They took my maps, but they left my notes lying on the ground. Couldn't read them, I guess."

"I can read," Amelina said, surprised at herself. "I can write, too."

"That's rare in these parts," Mr. Reed said. "You should be proud." His hand was pressed against his side again. "I feel like I might just live," he added, and smiled.

Amelina stared at him. He could write. She suddenly wanted to show him her own writing, to see if he could make it out. "Would you look at my practice book?" she asked. He nodded, and she jumped to her feet, upsetting the bucket. She caught it up and turned it over again. Then she ran to her room and got the book Father Le Blanc had given her.

The Yankee whistled through his teeth. "You have written a lot of pages here, Miss Carrett."

Amelina couldn't help smiling.

Mr. Reed began to read the last entry, the one she had made that very morning. She watched his lips twitch and she flushed, remembering how she had complained about having to write at all. When he handed the book back, he winked at her.

"I think you write real well. How long have you been at it?"

"Less than a year," she told him.

He nodded. "You're doing just fine."

Amelina took her book back. He pointed. "Look inside my hat."

She stood up and laid her book on the mantle next to the clock Nonc Alain had brought home, then bent to lift Mr. Reed's hat. Tucked into the crown was a packet wrapped in dark cloth. She took it out and undid it carefully. There was a thin stack of paper inside and a short stubby wooden pen. She had never seen anything like it before, and she turned it in her fingers.

"It's a pencil," he told her. "Made out of Tennessee cedarwood."

Amelina ran the dark gray tip of the pencil over her finger. It left a faint mark. She touched it to the paper.

"You have to draw it along," Mr. Reed said. "Try writing something."

Amelina reached for her journal and opened it to a blank page. *How can this work?* she wrote. And the script came out bold and dark and she laughed. "It doesn't drip like ink," she said, smiling at Mr. Reed.

"A real advantage for someone like you," he said wryly in his stilted French, and she laughed again.

"Did you learn your French in school?" Amelina asked him.

He shook his head. "No. I was raised by my grandmother. She was Acadian."

Amelina was stunned. "Acadian? Just like us?"

Mr. Reed was nodding, wincing as he shifted positions slightly. "They picked me for my French—said the Cajuns were all neutral and would help me."

Amelina nodded. "Most are, I think, but they don't want to help either side. My mother made me learn English."

Mr. Reed smiled. "I, too, was given no choice. My grandmère—" he began, then stopped, tilting his head.

"What?" Amelina asked him, but Mr. Reed held up one hand to silence her.

"I hear someone whistling," he said softly.

Amelina faced the door. "Nonc Alain," she whispered. "It has to be."

CHAPTER ELEVEN

The instant she said it, the door banged open. For a frozen second, Nonc Alain just stood still, water dripping from the edge of his long coat, his face a mask of astonishment. Then he lifted his gun.

"No!" Amelina shouted.

"What is this man doing here?" Nonc Alain demanded in French.

"He was hurt when I found him and I brought him here to have Tante Rosemarie help him," Amelina said, glancing back at the Yankee. "But he is better and . . ." She trailed off, uncertain what else to say.

Nonc Alain lowered the rifle barrel and closed the door behind himself. "He is wearing my clothes. Why?"

"His uniform was filthy," she blurted nervously, then realized her foolish mistake an instant too late.

The rifle came back up. "Uniform?"

Mr. Reed nodded and answered in French. "I am a soldier, sir."

Nonc Alain held the rifle steady. "And what commander do you fight under, sir?" He shook his head when Amelina began to speak. "No. Let him answer for himself, Amelina."

"I am an officer in the Union army," Mr. Reed said, clearly and evenly in French.

"Where is his gun?" Nonc Alain asked Amelina, ignoring the answer.

"I never saw one."

"I have no weapons," Mr. Reed affirmed, still speaking French. "They were taken away from me before I could escape."

"Ah!" Nonc Alain's brows shot up, his eyes widening. "You are the spy?"

Amelina glanced involuntarily at the papers in her hand and her uncle stepped closer, his rifle still slanting downward, pointing at Mr. Reed. "Read these papers to me, Amelina!"

She hesitated, then unfolded the first sheet. The letters were all familiar, but none of them seemed to make sense. "I can't," she said, puzzled, but relieved she couldn't.

"It's English, Amelina, not French," Mr. Reed told her.

Nonc Alain lifted his gun again. "Yankee, you will not speak to my niece with familiarity or any other way." He turned and looked at Amelina. "You have done me a favor," he said. "You are kindhearted,

Amelina, and that is a good thing in a girl. But war is for men. Go to your room now. And leave the papers here."

Amelina looked at Mr. Reed. He nodded slightly. She kept the pencil in her right palm as she handed over the papers with her left. Then she turned to the mantle and picked up her own journal. Nonc Alain frowned when he saw it, but he did not ask her why she had brought it out.

"Go, now!" Nonc Alain repeated.

Amelina crossed the room and opened her door, then glanced back. Nonc Alain was still staring at her. She lowered her head and went into her boudoir.

Sitting on her bed, Amelina was torn between crying and being angry. Nonc Alain left her to handle everything by herself, then he came home and took over without counting her feelings or opinions for anything. She fiddled with the strange little wooden pencil for a few seconds, then shoved it into her dress pocket and stood up. She blinked back her tears and went to the door when she heard Nonc Alain's voice.

"And my bed? The girl has given you my bed!" Nonc Alain was almost shouting.

Mr. Reed was harder to hear when he answered, and Amelina pressed her ear to the door. But whatever he said, it only made Nonc Alain more angry.

"You are right, Yankee," Nonc Alain said in his heavily accented English, ignoring the fact Mr. Reed had spoken to him in French. "She means no harm to anyone. Only good. She is going to become a nun when she is old enough."

Amelina caught her breath. He was saying it as though it were his decision and that he had made it.

Mr. Reed's voice rose again. "I apologize for coming into your home uninvited. I was weak and half frozen to death and I have a wound—"

Nonc Alain made a harsh sound. "The Yankee who eluded a bayonet thrust. They are still talking about how it missed you."

"Luck," Mr. Reed answered. "Or God's kindness."

"Do not speak of God to me," Nonc Alain said angrily. I am Catholic and—"

"So am I," Mr. Reed interrupted. "And an Acadian."

"That explains your French. But then why are you fighting for the Yankees?" Nonc Alain accused. "What sort of *chien* are you to fight with the Yankees?" Amelina could tell how angry her uncle was—he was calling Mr. Reed a dog.

Mr. Reed's voice dropped and his words came in bits and pieces, mostly impossible to understand. Amelina could tell he was explaining about his grandmother, telling Nonc Alain that he did not hate the South—that he only hated slavery.

There was a sudden silence from the front room.

Amelina pressed her ear to the door. Were they talking more quietly now? Outside, a long, low rumble of thunder announced the storm was not over yet. A half minute later, the thrumming of rain on the roof began, then intensified, making it impossible to hear what the men were saying to each other—if they were saying anything at all.

The sudden sound of footsteps, then a sharp rap on her door made Amelina spring backward. She just had time to sit on her bed as the door swung open.

"Listen to me," Nonc Alain said in a low voice, coming in and turning to close the door behind himself. "I have tied the Yankee's hands and feet together. I don't think he can go anywhere, but if you hear sounds in the night you must tell me." He wiped one hand across his face. "I have traveled since yesterday. I am too weary to do more before I sleep."

"What will you do with him?" Amelina asked quietly.

Nonc Alain waggled one finger back and forth, like a mother scolding a toddler. "That is not your concern."

Amelina's stomach tightened. "I like him."

Nonc Alain shrugged. "Young girls are foolish with their likes and dislikes."

Amelina stood up to face him. "If you hadn't come home tonight—"

"You would have awakened to find everything of

value gone from the house—the horse stolen, food, who knows what else. Or he might have hurt you."

"No," Amelina said flatly.

Nonc Alain arched his brows. "You cannot know how evil this Yankee is."

"When I first helped him, he told me not to because he thought I might get hurt."

Nonc Alain lifted his brows again and for the first time, Amelina could see he was listening.

Talking fast, Amelina told her uncle the whole story of helping the Yankee, including the long journey up the bayou with the marchand rowing along next to her, the reluctance of the Yankee to stain a borrowed shirt, his praise of her writing.

Nonc Alain listened without interrupting, but then he frowned and shrugged again. "But he is a spy, *ma chère*. I will take him to the Confederates tomorrow."

"Why are you helping them?" Amelina blurted out, and his face darkened.

"What a man does is not a little girl's affair," he said sternly.

Amelina took a step forward. "I am not a little girl."

"Of course you are," Nonc Alain said.

Amelina shook her head, angry. "Little girls don't live alone, taking care of a whole farm by themselves."

Nonc Alain glared at her and his response was so

close to what she had imagined she could almost recite it with him. "Are you a woman now? Are you my wife that you should speak to me so? *Non!* You are my niece, a little girl."

"But you are always gone," Amelina repeated. "Can you remember the last fish you caught for supper? The last field you plowed for corn or squash?"

Nonc Alain scowled at her a moment more, then turned toward the door. "If you hear noise from that room, you are to wake me. Do you understand?"

Amelina refused to nod, but there was no doubt she had heard him, no possible way to pretend she had not. "Why do you care about the Confederates?" she muttered, hoping he would hear her. He did. He looked at her over his shoulder.

"What?"

"You don't own slaves or care about the other things the Confederates say they are fighting for. You say slavery is wrong. So why would you help them?"

Nonc Alain turned slowly and stared into her eyes. "I do not care about any of it, you are right," he said. "I have been smiling at the Yankees and letting the Confederates think I am their friend at the same time."

Amelina stood very still. Suddenly, a lot of things made sense. He had not become a thief. Not exactly.

"Who gave you the pig?"

He smiled. "A sugar planter who thought I had

some sway with the Yankees and could protect his plantation from them. I did try to ask the captain if the place could be left alone . . . " Nonc Alain shrugged again. "The man owned many more pigs."

"And the clock?"

Nonc Alain smiled again. "I found it, lying beside the Opelousas Road, just that one little scratch in the base. No doubt some looting Yankee dropped it. War is full of opportunities, Amelina." He yawned.

Amelina felt almost sick and she wasn't quite sure why. What he was doing wasn't as wrong as what she had imagined he was doing. But it seemed worse somehow. "I want you to let Mr. Reed go." She said it as evenly and loudly as she could.

Nonc Alain stared at her in silence for a moment. "I will not. Catching a Yankee spy will convince the Confederates I am with them. They will stop watching to see where I go and what I do."

Amelina looked up at him. "Why would they watch you?"

"Because," he said slowly, his teeth clenched together in impatience, "they have seen me following along with the Yankees at times."

Amelina nodded. "Finding clocks and pigs."

He nodded emphatically. "But they think I could be selling secrets. Spying. Like your Yankee friend."

Amelina closed her eyes, trying to make sense of everything. It wasn't the same. Mr. Reed was a spy—

but he was also a good man who believed in what he was fighting for. Nonc Alain didn't care who won the war, so long as he got a little something out of the confusion.

"Your Yankee can sleep on the floor," Nonc Alain was saying. "It is early, but I have not slept in days. I am going to reclaim my bed." He looked at her harshly. "You have given away what was not yet yours to give, Amelina. This is still my house."

Amelina waited for him to turn and go out. Then she went to the door and opened it a little, just enough to see him asking Mr. Reed to move off the mattress. Mr. Reed did so, politely, wincing as he lay back down on the hard plank floor.

Amelina pushed the door shut as Nonc Alain turned toward her, waiting until she heard her uncle's bedroom door open and close. Then she waited a little longer to be sure he had gone to bed. Holding her breath, she pushed her door open and went out, her bare feet silent on the planks.

Both Nonc Alain and Mr. Reed might be asleep, but she could not end her day yet. She still had work to do.

CHAPTER TWELVE

Amelina peeked out first, able to see only a slanting path across the room and the closed back door. She listened. The house was silent except for the sounds of the storm from outside. The false dusk had fooled the stock into thinking it was evening. The cow was lowing as the sun sank toward the horizon and the chickens were clucking, waiting to be let into the coop for the night.

As Amelina stepped out of her room, she saw that Mr. Reed was lying in front of the hearth, his head on the spare pillow. His hands were bound together at his wrists—she couldn't see his feet. Nonc Alain had brought in a blanket as well, and had covered him. Amelina felt an ache go through her heart. Nonc Alain was not a bad man, nor was he cruel. Yet he was going to turn Mr. Reed over to men who would consider him an enemy. They might even kill him. War made so little sense.

Amelina went out to the cuisine. She plunged

her hands into the cool water and lifted the Yankee's dirty clothes, separating his uniform jacket from the rest. She set the shirt and trousers on the bench, sorry she didn't have enough time to wash them, too. She thrust the jacket beneath the water, slashing it back and forth in a rhythm that was as familiar to her as breathing.

"It isn't true," she whispered, answering her uncle at last. "I am not going to become a nun."

When the mud was dissolved and the water dark brown, Amelina dumped it, swinging the tub in a circle to avoid making another puddle on the already muddy ground. She wrung out the jacket, then carried the bucket to the cistern. Walking back and forth three times, she filled the second tub with clean water and lifted down the brown cake of laundry soap she had made a month before. She sliced off pieces of it with the soap knife, working each slippery crescent with her hand beneath the water until it dissolved. Then she set to work once more, plunging the jacket beneath the water.

When the water was dirty, she dumped it again and wrung the jacket out, then refilled the tub with rinse water. It was raining and she had no need to conserve their water now, she told herself, knowing that even if the day had been dry, she would have filled the tub high. She wanted Mr. Reed's jacket *clean*.

Amelina hurried. Carrying the washed, wrung-out jacket over her arm, Amelina tiptoed back into the house, looking first at Nonc Alain's door. It was still closed tightly. She crossed to the hearth and carefully set more wood on top of the coals. As the flames leaped upward, Amelina hung the blue jacket on the clothes peg nearest the fire. Using slender sticks of kindling, she propped the jacket open so it would dry quickly.

The cow lowed again, and Amelina hurried silently out the back door. She got the milk bucket from its hook in the cuisine and went out into the yard.

Vagabond and his hens were gathered around the coop door as she passed, as eager to get in now as they had been to get out that morning. Amelina counted before she opened the door. There were fifteen hens and the young rooster. All were here, safe and sound. They clucked and bobbed their heads as they hurried each other along, hopping up to their perch rails almost immediately.

The mother hen that had been shut in all day came clucking out, her babies behind the wide skirt of her broad tail feathers. She scratched at the ground, agitated and flustered, then, seeing the storm dusk, she regathered her family and went straight back into the coop. But she stayed near the door, still clucking, looking outside as if she was considering coming back out.

Amelina laughed, shaking her head. "That is

exactly how I feel," she told the hen. "What is the right thing to do?" Then, waiting as the hen resettled her family in the deep rice straw behind the perches, Amelina made a decision. She had probably already made it, she knew, or she would not have hurried to wash out Mr. Reed's jacket, but she was just now getting around to admitting to herself what she was going to do. Nonc Alain was wrong. There were things here she did own.

She made quick work of milking the cow and setting the brimming glass bowl in the water bucket. The pigs would have to wait. She ran around the side of the house toward the dock.

Her pirogue had been her father's. That meant it was hers to give as a gift. The oar, too. Her father had carved it from cypress with his own hands. These things were her inheritance: these and the things in her trunk.

Amelina ran swiftly all the way to the end of the dock. Stepping into her boat, she sat on the narrow plank bench and bent forward to sweep up the stray bits of moss that littered the bottom. When she was finished, she held her oar across her lap for a few minutes, wondering what her father would think of this. He might understand. He might not.

"Is that you, Miss Carrett?"

The marchand's voice startled Amelina so badly she very nearly upset her boat springing up to face him. He was still a little ways down the bayou, calling to her. Amelina leaned to untie her mooring, then turned her pirogue in one smooth motion and rowed toward him to keep him from shouting again—and waking Nonc Alain.

"Where are you going so late in the evening?" Amelina asked quietly when she got close enough.

He touched his hat. "Does that bateau mean that your uncle got home?"

Amelina nodded.

"I am relieved," Mr. Sawyer said, "though your aunt and uncle say you are used to him being gone by now. Your cousin said she admires you."

"Perrine said that?" Amelina asked, astonished.

Mr. Sawyer nodded. "Oh, yes. They are proud. They say you are running the place more or less."

Amelina sat a little straighter. "I manage."

Mr. Sawyer smiled. "When the rain let up I thought I'd get a little ways south if I could. I know some folks a few miles down I can stay with if it gets bad again."

Amelina nodded and he went right on. "Your aunt fed me a wonderful supper," Mr. Sawyer said. "Your cousin Perrine asked me to look in on you on my way past. She said to tell you she is sorry." He smiled. "She wouldn't say what for."

Amelina smiled back at him, relieved and grateful to Perrine, but fighting an impulse to look toward the house. If Nonc Alain did awaken, her plan was ruined. "Thank you, sir," she said. Then she straightened her spine and lifted her chin. "Bon voyage," she said politely. "I will hope for your safe travel."

"I thank you," he said, just as politely. "Tell your uncle I ran into a bateau of Confederate boys headed upstream, trying to catch a Yankee spy. I asked about the gunfire we heard. They said there was a battle today down on Buzzard's Prairie below Opelousas."

Amelina nodded solemnly, thinking about the wound in Mr. Reed's chest. It was nothing compared to the kinds of wounds many others would have gotten today, then. How many lay hurt and alone right now? How many had died?

"Tell him this, too," Mr. Sawyer said, picking up his oars again. "Those three boys were wearing blue—Union coats! Said they raided some Yankee camp for clothes. Got some Enfield rifles, too." He shook his head. "I almost took a shot at 'em before they called out to me."

He lowered his oars and nodded at her. Amelina maneuvered out of his way and waved as he passed her, rowing at a steady pace. As he disappeared into the gathering dusk, she heard the popping of distant gunfire and wondered if it had been there all along and she just hadn't noticed it. Were they still fighting, then? She paddled back toward the dock, feeling sad, but knowing what she had to do.

Once she was back inside, Amelina went to her trunk and took out her father's clothes. There was a thick cottonade shirt her mother had made, and the trousers Papa had worn to dance in, barely worn. Amelina pulled them out and folded them, then slipped back out. Laying them down, she went to the cuisine for a kitchen knife.

"Mr. Reed," she whispered, touching his cheek lightly. He twisted, coming awake with a start. In the firelight she saw him pass through a twilight of panic before he recognized her. She showed him the knife. "Hurry," she whispered, and he raised his bound hands.

Amelina threw the cut rope into the fire, then gestured toward the clothing. "My father's," she told him in a low voice. "Mine to give."

He nodded, seeming to understand her perfectly. Amelina stood up and went out the back door, grabbing a candle from the shelf. She wrapped up salt pork and a day's-old corn bread in clean rags, wishing she had something better to offer him. Then she turned and went back into the house.

Mr. Reed was standing, dressed in her father's clothes. Nonc Alain's were lying neatly folded to one side of the hearth, safe from popping embers. Mr. Reed gestured toward his uniform coat. "Thank you."

"There are Confederates on the bayou dressed up like Yankees," Amelina told him, repeating the marchand's story in a whisper.

Mr. Reed nodded. "I'll hide my jacket and speak French if I run into any birds wearing the wrong feathers."

Gesturing for him to follow, Amelina led him out the front door. Halfway to the dock, they both heard the distant gunfire.

"I will get your uncle's bateau back to him if I can. You can tell him I forced you to free me, that I stole—"

Amelina shook her head. "I will tell him I gave you my father's clothes and his pirogue and that they were gifts."

Mr. Reed reached out to shake her hand, as though she were a man. "Thank you, Amelina. I owe you my life. I will get someone to bring the pirogue back if I possibly can."

Amelina blinked back tears as he stepped into the pirogue and sat on the bench to pick up the oar. She heard him take in a quick gasp of breath and knew it would hurt him terribly to paddle.

He did not call out a farewell, but she saw him turn and lay the paddle across his lap, facing her to lift both hands as though he was praying. Then he disappeared into the dusk.

Amelina started back toward the house, knowing she would not be able to sleep at all this night. As she crawled into her bed, she could not stop her reeling thoughts.

Mr. Sawyer was a good man who had been genuinely concerned for her safety. Mr. Reed's good heart had made her miss her father. Nonc Alain was only trying to get by, to keep a little of the wealth the war was setting adrift. Were all the soldiers like them? How could so many good men agree to have a war?

Nearly midnight, and I am still too full of thoughts to sleep. Since I did not write in my book earlier while Perrine was still here, I will write in it now.

There is no lack of news to write this day. I will start at the beginning. I am using Mr. Reed's pencil to write this and already much prefer it to the steel pen.

Nonc Alain woke at sunrise. Oh! He was angry with me. He rowed away and was gone for several hours. I know he was determined to bring Mr. Reed back, but he could not find him. I said prayers, I admit it. I want nothing more than for this war to be over, for all the good men to go home safe and sound. I want to stop being afraid.

Perrine came midmorning and I had to explain to her where my pirogue had gone, then where Nonc Alain had gone. She understood me, I think, at the end of the tale, though not at the beginning. She says if she is ever in trouble, she hopes I am the one to come upon her. We had a very good day gardening together, talking as we worked. We made up our argument and she said she could understand my touchiness. I hope so. Perrine is an honored and valued friend. I wish to remain close hearts until we are both gray headed and wrinkled.

Nonc Alain growled and groused his way around us for an hour or two after he got home, but late this afternoon he began cleaning the harness and the plow.

I dared not ask him if he intended to turn the fallow fields, but it is my hope he will do just that. I am saying more prayers.

Two good things happened today after Perrine left. Nonc Alain said good night, and he told me he intends to stay here more—I think he might be afraid I will bring more Yankees home! Whatever his reason is, I am glad. I could tell he has forgiven me. Even if he had not, I would not be sorry I helped the Yankee escape, but I am relieved that he has.

The second good thing was this: Beneath my pillow was a note. Only a few words, written overlarge with charcoal from the fire, on a page torn from this book. It said, "Thank you, Amelina. Yrs, Michael Reed. P.S. Write me a letter after the war."

And he wrote down his address. I have put it in the bottom of my trunk and I will practice my writing so he will be able to read my letter when it arrives at his door. I will pray for his safety, and for the end of this terrible war. And now, having told the story all through, perhaps I can sleep.

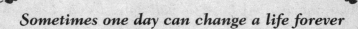

Sometimes one day can change a life forever

American Diaries

Different girls,
living in different periods of America's past
reveal their hearts' secrets in the pages
of their diaries. Each one faces a challenge
that will change her life forever.
Don't miss any of their stories:

SURVIVAL

Would you get out alive?

FACED WITH DISASTER, ORDINARY PEOPLE FIND UNTAPPED DEPTHS OF COURAGE AND DETERMINATION THEY NEVER DREAMED THEY POSSESSED.

Find Adventure in these books!

#1 TITANIC

On a clear April night hundreds of passengers on the *Titanic* find themselves at the mercy of a cold sea. Few will live to remember the disaster—will Gavin and Karolina be among the survivors?

#2 EARTHQUAKE

Can two strangers from very different worlds work together to survive the terror of the quake—crumbling buildings, fire, looting, and chaos?

#3 BLIZZARD

Can a Rocky Mountain rancher's daughter and her rich, spoiled cousin stop arguing long enough to cooperate to survive a sudden, vicious blizzard?

#4 FIRE

Fate and fire throw Nate and Julie together on the dark streets of Chicago. Now they must find a way out before the flames spreading across the city cut off their only chance of escape!

ALSO:
#5 FLOOD
#6 DEATH VALLEY

NEW!
#7 CAVE-IN
#8 TRAIN WRECK
#9 HURRICANE

COMING SOON!
#10 FOREST FIRE
#11 SWAMP